Provenance Unknown

sands press
Brockville, Ontario

Provenance Unknown

Sonia Nicholson

sands press

sands press

A Division of 3244601 Canada Inc.
300 Central Avenue West
Brockville, Ontario
K6V 5V2

Toll Free 1-800-563-0911 or 613-345-2687
http://www.sandspress.com

ISBN 978-1-990066-24-5
Copyright © Sonia Nicholson
All Rights Reserved

For information on bulk purchases of this book or any book published by Sands Press, please call 1-800-563-0911.

To book an author for your live event, please call: 1-800-563-0911

Sands Press is a literary publisher interested in new and established authors wishing to develop and market their product. For more information please visit our website at www.sandspress.com.

This is a book over ten years in the making. A huge thank you to Sands Press for championing the story I carried for a long time, and to my editor Laurie Carter for her "tough love".

Sincerest thanks are due to my faithful and trusted alpha readers Cheryl Plaskett and Paul Nicholson, my son. Cheryl, my high school co-author, also provided valuable insight into adoption, and character psychology. My mom Angelina Resendes and sister Sylvia Nesbitt gave endless encouragement and some very helpful plot suggestions. Thank you to my husband Brent Nicholson for his love, support, and patience, and for the week we spent together in the Pereire neighbourhood of Paris; and to my daughter Rose for sharing creative time and motivating me with her own work.

I owe much to my beta readers Adam Montgomery, Stewart Harding, Sylvia Nesbitt, Douglas Nicholson, and Jenny Dekteroff. The wonderful ladies of the Maplewood Writers' Collective gave me the kickstart I needed to pull out all the legwork I had done a decade earlier and finally start writing, and the archivists writing group of which I am a member provided constructive feedback in the querying process.

Much gratitude to my archive colleagues past and present, particularly my mentor Caroline Duncan. I would not be where I am in my career now without her guidance. A special shoutout to Saanich Archives for confirming and clarifying local historical details.

Finally, my humblest thanks to the City of Light and to the Beatles—especially Paul McCartney, after whom my son is named—for the inspiration.

In gratitude for those who came before,
and in love for those who will follow.

« Il dépend de celui qui passe
Que je sois tombe ou trésor,
Que je parle ou me taise,
Ceci ne tient qu'à toi
Ami, n'entre pas sans désir »

It depends on those who pass
Whether I am a tomb or treasure
Whether I speak or am silent
The choice is yours alone.
Friend, do not enter without desire.
— Paul Valéry

Inscribed on the Palais de Chaillot, Paris

CHAPTER 1

On nights such as this, when it seems the whole world has succumbed to stillness, I walk with ghosts. While seasonal peace reigns in the hearts of mankind, I allow myself a private moment to ache, to grieve. Edith is sleeping in the next room. Like the fire in the hearth, her face illuminates the darkness. I chide myself for my weakness; the little angel needs me to carry on with the same resolution that has brought us through the difficulties of the last few years. She must not read any concern on my face.

We attended Christmas Mass yesterday at St. Andrew's. Instead of one candle, we lit two. Edith and I sat silently in the church after the service and did not leave until both flames had finally fallen to blackness. They struggled as both of you struggled, in your own ways, and I too, now, feel myself dwindling. The light seems dim, indeed.

* * *

Sunday, August 9, 2009

The story did not make sense. Or at the least, it was highly unrealistic. What kind of self-respecting historian spent their time treasure hunting? Stealing the U.S. Declaration of Independence? Ridiculous. Even though she'd only worked in the archives for a couple of years, Michele knew that taking original records was not only a crime, it went against the core of the profession's ethics. It simply wasn't done, no matter how good the reason. Standards aside, the history in the movie was seriously flawed. There was just enough of a splattering of actual facts to make it seem accurate, but really, the plot was outrageous. Reality and proper procedure be damned! And yet, she found it hard to turn away.

Truth be told, she'd watched *National Treasure* a few times since it came out in 2004, and it just may have given her the idea to pursue work in the archival field. In her defence, she wasn't the only one of her colleagues in Greater Victoria (or beyond, for that matter) to indulge in watching it. It was a more common guilty pleasure than any of them cared to admit. In public, archivists scoffed at these sorts of misrepresentations. Though only an assistant, she was a professional now too, right? But that didn't mean abandoning her secret admiration for Ben Gates. His passion, fearlessness, and brazen disregard for order only made him more intriguing. Maybe the appeal of the whole thing, she mused, lay precisely in the lack of reason. There was something about the escape, the adventure …

A crash interrupted her reverie, followed by a flash of red. "Here comes Spider-Man!" Henry had raced down the wooden steps in his web-patterned pyjamas. They were too short, she noted with a sigh. The bright blanket-cape was a creative touch, though. Reluctantly, but with the speed that comes with practice, she turned off the DVD player and dropped the remote control onto the coffee table. It was time to put on her maternal hat.

"Sweetheart, you're supposed to be sleeping." She rose from the couch and her knees cracked. The clock on the wall read 10:00 p.m.

Henry, unconcerned with trivial matters like bedtime, blinked his startlingly grey eyes at her. "But Mummy, I was playing Spider-Man and I wanted to save you."

She studied her son from his toes to his cowlick. He was not a baby anymore and sometimes she hardly recognized him. Henry was a "big boy" now—he insisted—growing every day into mysterious features she didn't recognize. He didn't take after her, except for maybe the medium-brown hair. She was fairly sure there was no resemblance to his father, as far as she could remember from that hazy union five years ago. No, Henry was uniquely himself, a curious mash-up of childhood frivolity and worn concern, the type usually acquired through years and experience. Here she was, still in denial over her thirtieth birthday, while he regularly channeled someone twice her age. And he hadn't even started kindergarten yet.

Not yet, but soon. Michele had been dreading school shopping, planning to put it off as long as possible. Even with the sales advertised in the newspaper flyers, all the supplies seemed pricey and the list pretty long. Why did kids need so much—stuff? It was shocking. Wasn't it just a pencil, eraser, and some crayons? To buy all the required items would add up. She winced thinking about it but then shook her head. Somehow she would figure it out, just as she always had. News reports from earlier in the summer had declared the recession over, so the economy should be on the upswing soon. Maybe the archives would finally expand its hours. She could only hope. She was grateful to have landed a city job with good pay and benefits, but the part-time status made living in a place as expensive as Victoria, British Columbia, all the more difficult.

As Michele herded Henry back up to the tiny sleeping area they shared, she averted the even stare of the parson's table below. But her mind still saw what her eyes had avoided: precarious piles of envelopes containing notices and warnings. Just past the table on the cracked yellow kitchen wall clung a calendar, and she knew without going to look that there were five more days until her next pay day. The situation felt like being lost in the desert. The cheque would not bring rescue; it would provide the type of relief you feel when finding a few more drops of water at the bottom of the canteen. Thirst temporarily quenched, yes, but still nothing but sand in every direction.

She slumped. With a brave face she tucked Henry into bed, resisting his protests. He continued to insist he had to save her. "Thank you, Spider-Man, but even heroes have to crash once in a while." A goodnight kiss later, she returned downstairs.

After narrowing her eyes at the table for a moment, she diverted her attention to the living room and studied the space: the scraped-up fir floors, the dented panelling, the chipped beams. The house's weary bones creaked with effort, but the structure still carried a certain dignity. It wasn't grand now, and even in its heyday it wouldn't have been considered fancy. It looked like a simple farmhouse, with its A-frame roof and small porch off the front door.

There wasn't much information at the archives on the building (one of the first things she had looked up when she started her job), but it was built in 1918. She had learned from working on an inquiry that quite a number of houses had been constructed after the First World War on what was now Rutledge Park. She would often look at it from her upper floor window of the Alder Street house where she lived and imagine the tidy layout of the new subdivision, with the orchards that were common in the Cloverdale neighbourhood visible up the slope. Whether or not the house had originally been part of this development, rather than a farm, it had been home to many residents over time. According to the old city directories, it had been occupied through its history by a succession of farmers, brick layers, cobblers, electricians and cooks. Labourers, working people.

Like her landlady, Mrs. Eliades. Michele could hear her in the depths of the kitchen humming along to the Everly Brothers on the oldies station. She was most certainly sitting in the middle of the room on one of the 1970s vinyl kitchen chairs, opposite an identical one where a plastic tub caught peeled potatoes or cradled bread dough. Mrs. Eliades always cooked and baked late at night, stockpiling her finished products in a small deep freezer. Apparently, her beloved Dimitri had first fallen in love with the pastries before the woman, and she still made them two years after his death in quantities enough to fill a bomb shelter.

To make money she cleaned houses, scrubbing floors on hands and knees with the diligence typical of the Old Country. She looked much older than sixty-seven, but she never spoke of retiring, or of moving to a more affordable market. Michele was acutely aware of how expensive it was to live in Victoria. Why else would this independent Greek woman rent her upstairs and share her living room and kitchen with a tenant? Michele suspected there was another reason she stayed, however. In the time Michele, and later Henry, had lived there, it was obvious Mrs. Eliades and her husband had spent decades of their lives together in that house, and now that he was gone, it was all she had left of him. It was clear she would do whatever it took to keep it. But while the thought of leaving must have been too much for Mrs. Eliades to bear, Michele couldn't help but analyze not only the financial but also the emotional cost. Wouldn't it be harder to stay and face the memories on a daily basis? If it were her in that position, she was pretty sure she would be out the door and getting herself away from the pain as fast as possible. It was counterproductive to stick around.

As the last notes of "Devoted to You" died, she felt pity for Mrs. Eliades—but also gratitude. This woman was trapped in the past, in a time she could never get back. But it was this stubborn nostalgia that had, in a way, given Michele a place to live. When the time had come for Dimitri to move to long term care after his cancer diagnosis, his wife, known for her practicality, had made the decision then and there to open her home. She needed income and had extra space, and Victoria had a lot of students and not enough places to house them. As it happened, Michele had been relentlessly researching rentals online and had come across the minimalist ad minutes after it had been posted. "Upstairs room and bath for clean student in beautiful house. No party, no mess. Beside park. Available now." She'd responded right away and offered to come for an interview that same day. She had presented herself to Mrs. Eliades and hoped her efficient, reliable, and neat-freak self would be enough to get her the place, given that she didn't have any previous landlords to use as references. Mrs. Eliades had looked her over, hands on hips, and pronounced in her heavy accent, "You seem like a nice girl. You no party or make mess in my house and we not gonna have a problem. When you can move in?" And that was that. Michele had gone back to Amanda's place to pack.

Mrs. Eliades was singing along off-key to the next song when Michele's mind returned to the present. She peeked around the doorway into the kitchen and watched. The woman was not just a landlady. Mrs. Eliades—Maria—had been there through Michele's university graduation, the unexpected pregnancy, and the first years of motherhood, providing advice (wanted or not), homemade meals, and regular babysitting. In fact, she had been Henry's only caregiver while Michele had been at school and now while she was at work at the City Archives. He thought of her as a grandmother, particularly since he didn't have a "real" one of his own. Mrs. Eliades, whom he called Didi, was just fine as a substitute. She'd been so generous and there was really no way Michele could ever repay that kindness. Which made her feel all the worse about her current money-flow situation; or more accurately, lack thereof.

One phone call. That's all it would take for Amanda to help out in any way she could. She had always been fiercely loyal. Protective by nature. Michele could recall an incident from kindergarten when Kyle had stolen, probably inadvertently, her snow boots from the cloakroom cubby. Amanda had wandered in to find Michele in tears, assessed the situation, and promptly clocked poor Kyle square on the nose. She hadn't caused any serious harm but there had been quite a bit of blood, which meant the medical room for Kyle and the Principal's office for Amanda. Her parents John and Barbara were called, and when everything was all said and done, she had come away with a stern lecture, an order to apologize, and no TV for a week, (which because they shared the recreation room in the basement meant no TV for Michele either).

She smiled. It wasn't funny, really, but she couldn't help it. It was such an Amanda thing to do. Michele missed those days more and more of late. The two of them still spoke on the phone or video chatted once in a while, but so much had changed since they were growing up together. She was still on Vancouver Island, and Amanda lived a day's drive away in Kelowna with her husband and three kids. A beautiful, loving family. Michele didn't want to bother her with her problems. She could deal with them alone.

There were John and Barbara, of course. But his mobility was in decline and she had been suffering from dementia for a number of years. Michele couldn't bring herself to ask them for money now. She had never called them Mom and Dad—though they had legally adopted her—but they were everything anyone could ever ask for in parents. Better than her biological ones, transients who had left her at Sacred Heart when she was little; she'd been too young to remember them. No matter. John and Barbara had accepted her and loved her like their own. And living with them meant that her best friend was her sister, too. What more could a girl want?

When Michele turned ten, John and Barbara had sat her down one evening and broached the subject of her family. Maybe now that she was getting older, she might be curious about where she came from, they had suggested, sitting hand in hand on the couch and facing her with tears in their eyes. Maybe she wanted to learn about them. She carried their last name, after all. "Enough time has passed," Barbara had said to John.

But Michele was not interested. "No thank you, I'm good," she'd responded, darting out of the room before they could say anything more. They had tried again occasionally after that, but eventually the span between attempts got longer and longer until they had stopped altogether. Her answer had always been the same.

Her parents hadn't wanted her. Period. It was clear from the story John and Barbara had told her. Parents who abandoned their children didn't deserve them, so why would she want to know those strangers? To have a relationship with them? They passed through town and out of her life. Permanently. She didn't miss that so-called family.

John, Barbara, and Amanda were all she had needed, and she never wanted them to change their minds about keeping her. Which is why she'd never told them about the images that flickered in her mind as if they were being shown on a faulty projector. They came rarely and unexpectedly, like a few playing cards that had been separated from the rest of the deck long ago. No one ever knew about the pink stuffed bunny and the plastic highchair with the metal buckle cold to the touch. About the blue apron that swung from side to side in a slow, steady rhythm. About the faint echo of a woman's laughter, getting farther and farther away each time. And always there was the music, bits and pieces of notes and words and a voice. It was a disjointed series of colours and sounds that for all she knew she had picked up from TV. They might not even belong to her at all. Certainly not worth mentioning.

Suddenly she heard a much closer voice. Mrs. Eliades appeared in front of her, wiping her hands on a dish towel. The corners of her mouth turned down at a sharp angle that made Michele uneasy.

"I am glad you are here, Michele. You are so busy girl all the time. I need to talk with you about something."

"Oh, um, yes. I've just been so swamped lately. With work. You know …" She shifted from foot to foot. She had a feeling this was the beginning of a conversation she didn't want to have.

Mrs. Eliades seemed to fill the entire kitchen doorway as she spoke. "Michele, is already more than a week since the first day of the month. I know is hard for you, but …"

Michele took a step back. No, definitely not what she wanted to discuss right now. "You know, I was actually just about to head out. For my run. I couldn't make it earlier tonight and I'm just really needing to get that workout in."

"But you no have running shoes, no exercise clothes." Mrs. Eliades raised her right eyebrow to an impressive height.

"Oh, that." Michele glanced down at her jeans and her cream ballet flats. *Just be cool*, she thought. "These are actually… stretchy jeans. They look normal but double as workout pants. And these shoes are so much more comfortable for running. More natural for the feet." She plastered on a smile that she hoped didn't seem as fake as it felt. Mrs. Eliades' facial expression eased up a little. She was about to respond but Michele jumped in first. "It's getting pretty late so I really should get going. No need to wait up or anything. And Henry's finally sound asleep, so he won't be any trouble at all." She'd eased herself through the living room and was now only a few feet from the front door.

Mrs. Eliades relented. "OK, but we really need to talk. We sit down tomorrow." It was a statement, not a question.

Michele forced a wave as she bolted out the door and down the steps. She paused at the bottom, placed her hands on her thighs, and tilted her torso forward. Then she blew a long, slow breath out towards the concrete. Turning to the right, she jogged around the corner of the house to the pedestrian shortcut that led into Rutledge Park.

In the confines of the abandoned tennis court, a fluffy Bichon chased a ball and appeared as a blaze of white across the green surface. The court was usually occupied all day in the summer but at this time of night most people were home in bed, getting ready to start a new work week. Which is where she should have been too, but she had needed to get away while she could. She had to buy some time. The dog's owner, an older man, turned and gave her a slight nod. He, too, was part of the exclusive club of neighbours that found solace in the night.

She returned the greeting as if it were a secret handshake and then continued her half-hearted sprint, stopping at the playground. The metal slide and the chains of the swings reflected the amber park lighting. If she squinted her eyes just right, she could almost imagine the equipment as chairs and tables at a cafe with strings of lights surrounding them. Like Van Gogh's *The Cafe Terrace*. She stole through the playground to reach her favourite part, the pink concrete elephant that was the park's signature feature. After checking that no one was watching, she clambered up onto Rutley's back and let her knees settle into the groove behind his ears.

It was silly, but she always made a point of making contact with the elephant every time she was in the park: when she was pushing Henry on the swings or letting him play in the gravel with his cars; when she was hurrying to catch a bus up on Douglas Street; when she was indeed going for a run. Rutley, with his black eyes painted on a bit crooked and his half-open mouth, was always there waiting to greet her no matter what was going on in her life. Michele nearly broke out laughing. Was it wrong for a grown woman to feel attached to a statue meant for children to climb? She could admit to herself that she often didn't feel like an adult. She could live with twenty-three or thirteen or even three, but she could not accept thirty. Would a thirty-year old give this pachyderm a pat every time they passed? Would a thirty-year old be sitting on top of him alone at eleven at night hiding from their problems? She didn't think so.

A breeze came up and brought goosebumps to her bare arms. It had been a pleasant twenty-one degrees Celsius during the day so she had worn her camisole tank top, but now the temperature had dipped a few degrees. She wasn't ready to go home yet, though. Perhaps she should *actually* get a workout, even though she didn't have the right gear on. She had lied about going for a run but the part about needing exercise had been true. Besides, it would warm her up. She slid off Rutley and stretched at the playground before jogging out of the park. She headed south on Rutledge Street, accelerating as the road climbed. The jeans were not ideal, but not as bad as she had thought they would be. She moved faster, passing the houses on the left and apartment buildings on the right. Most of the windows were dark and no one but her was outside. Sweat broke out on her forehead and under her arms and she pushed harder until the buildings blurred. Her feet were already sore; the thin ballet flats made it feel like she was running barefoot. When she reached Tolmie Avenue, she paused only long enough to navigate left for the short block to Glasgow Avenue. She continued back northward, down the hill and past the Scout Hall to Inverness Road.

When she read the street sign, Michele remembered that a few roads in the neighbourhood had Scottish names because of the Scots that had settled there. The most notable was Dr. William Fraser Tolmie. A doctor with the famed Hudson's Bay Company, Tolmie was born in Inverness and did his medical studies at the University of Glasgow. One of the original European landowners in the Victoria area, he had appropriately named both his prominent stone residence and his farm—over one-thousand clover-covered acres of hills and valleys—Cloverdale. According to one article she'd read at the archives, the landscape had likely reminded him of home.

Whenever she was out, she tried to picture the land as Tolmie had seen it. She could visualize what his view would have been from his house on the hill, looking out over the fields towards the fledgling city of Victoria and the mountains. She thought about what it might have been like for Tolmie's sons and daughters to grow up here in such a well-known family. One son, Simon Fraser, later became Premier of British Columbia. In the account he wrote of his father and of Cloverdale, he described the daily schedule: the children went to bed at nine at night and were up at five, beginning the day with their studies. Tolmie Sr. must have been a tough, strict man, but an extremely intelligent one too. She found the family fascinating.

She had continued running along Inverness Road to Cloverdale Avenue and now she slowed down as she approached Alder Street. Thinking about history was always invigorating, but now she had to get back to reality. She peered ahead to her place and breathed a sigh of relief. It looked like all of the lights were out, including the one in the kitchen. Mrs. Eliades had gone to bed. Sweaty and alert, Michele approached the house. The front steps didn't creak but she tiptoed her way up anyway, stopping on the porch. She sat down on the top step and gave a heavy exhale. The moon was on its way from full to half, still shining just enough in the clear sky to cast her shadow around her. She dropped her head into her now-clammy hands. Despite having avoided the conversation this time, she knew what Mrs. Eliades wanted to discuss. It had to be about money. The rent was late, again, and Michele hadn't paid her share of the utility bills. *What am I going to do?* She had racked her brain in the middle of many sleepless nights for possible solutions, and come up empty. For the shortest of moments, she let the loneliness come.

Just as quickly the sky clouded over and she stiffened, resolute. She unlocked the door with the key from her pocket and slipped inside. In the darkness, the furniture stood like the Chinese Terracotta Army guarding a tomb. She felt her way through the living room while her eyes adjusted. Even though she was careful, she banged her thigh into the corner of the parson's table, making the stack of mail teeter like an advanced game of Jenga. "Ouch!" Her right hand shot to her thigh to rub the spot; a bruise was already blooming. She reached out her left hand to try and steady herself and the table. Meanwhile the mail pile leaned and shifted, and she could only watch as the envelopes were flung into the air and past her face before floating to the hardwood. "Shoot, shoot, shoot." She scrambled onto the floor, sliding her hands along it to gather the pieces. She shuffled them together and set them back on the table. Her general coordination level left much to be desired, but the timing on this latest example could have been better. Plus, she didn't need another reminder of her problems.

Her pulse still coming down after that rush of adrenaline, she raised an ear and listened for anyone stirring. The last thing she wanted was Henry or Mrs. Eliades waking up at this hour. There was nothing from any of the bedrooms, however, and the silence was reassuring. Michele's ears were still vigilant, and the sounds of the house came into sharp focus: the clock ticking, the walls settling as the outside temperature cooled, the fridge buzzing as it kicked on. But under those, something else came through. Was that music? She listened again, perplexed. There it was: the faintest of melodies drifting from the kitchen. She relaxed, realizing Mrs. Eliades must not have turned the knob on her old radio all the way down to the off position. Michele followed the sound through the doorway and past the appliances to the small table at the back of the room. Bending down, she confirmed her suspicion. Yes, that was all it was. She smiled a little. It really was sweet the way Mrs. Eliades always played her oldies while she worked. Michele, better able to see through the darkness now, brought her hand towards the brown knob. Just as her fingers took hold of it, the next song began.

The unmistakable notes made her freeze on the spot. Like an instrument luring an asp out of a wicker basket, the guitar played the opening she recognized. Each time a string was plucked, the notes reverberated through her. She lowered her body as they descended in that quick scale. Paul McCartney's smooth voice sang the title, "Michelle ...", and the walls caved in around her. She curled into a ball on the checkerboard floor like a game piece in danger of being taken. Her eyes closed and she saw the blue apron, swaying and spinning and getting closer. The woman's voice faded in and out, trying to make its way to the surface. Michele called out a weak "No" and shook her head, fists clenched. It was happening again, but she would put a stop to it. The French portion of the lyrics began, and she opened her hands and pressed them down hard against the cold floor. She pushed herself to her knees, stopped, tried to slow her shallow breathing. The song reached the bridge. She opened her eyes, threw her arm up, and felt for the knob. When she'd found it, she spun it to the left until she heard the merciful click. Those thirty-five seconds had seemed like a lifetime.

Michele took in the sweet silence. She remained in a trance on her knees, rooted to a black square on the linoleum. Bit by bit she became aware of her surroundings: the small table directly in her line of sight, the white vintage stove, the blue ceramic mixing bowl on the counter. *Find three things.* She concentrated on them and began to calm down. It wasn't a perfect method, but it helped. Her whole body was stiff, and it slowed her as she pushed herself up to standing. It had aged years in the time that had passed. She hadn't heard the song in so long, but it still had the same bizarre effect. With every "incident," as she referred to them, just the beginning of the melody was enough to send her spiralling. When the images and sounds had gone, it always seemed like they had been a dream, scraps of mismatched fabric and thread thrown together to form a piece both familiar and odd. The most frustrating part was that she had no idea why the song made her so upset. She hadn't told anyone about any of it. How could she explain to others something she didn't understand herself? And, she admitted, she was embarrassed. It was weird and unsettling and quite frankly, she didn't want to talk about it.

She didn't have time for this nonsense, either, she reminded herself. There were more pressing matters to deal with, like work, and Henry, and money: The Big Three. She shuffled out of the kitchen in slow motion. It was nearly midnight. She dragged her feet through the living room without even looking at the mail. When she reached the bottom of the stairs, she took hold of the antique finial on the newel post. Its smooth, solid surface felt comforting in the palm of her hand, almost like it could speak to her and share the stories it had witnessed over one hundred years. History could be weird and unsettling, but unlike her personal experiences, it made sense to her. It made the world make sense. Michele pulled herself up the staircase using the railing for support and then trudged into the dark bedroom. If she could, she would transport herself up through the sloped ceiling and fly away through the night sky.

How would it feel to be lighter, to be free? To go out on the town on a weekday evening just because she could. To do all the things that the girls she had known in school had been doing in their twenties and now into their thirties? What would it be like to check out different clubs and dance all night? To travel through Europe one summer and get lost more than once? Where would she have ended up if she'd been given the opportunity? What would her life be like now if she had gone on adventures, had fun, fallen in love? She sat on the bed, careful not to wake her son. She did love him, she thought as she watched his sleeping form, his small frame rising and falling. But having him had changed everything. Her so-called friends—except for Amanda, of course—had dispersed when Michele had gotten pregnant. They were still young and vibrant, and a single mom just hadn't fit in with their lifestyle. She had still been figuring out how to look after herself when she had become responsible for someone else's care too. A helpless, innocent baby with no one else in the world and dependent on her alone. It had been a heavy load. It still was.

Henry turned and she held her breath, not moving a muscle. He tugged on his Spider-Man top, flipped his covers away, and returned to his deep sleep, a smile flickering across his flushed face. *He must be having a good dream.* A deep guilt pierced her heart like a knife. What was she doing, filling her brain with all these crazy ideas? She chalked it up to the day she'd had. Those ideas were in the past; all of those doors were closed to her and she had to move on. Of course Henry had to be the priority. Everything else had to be filed away. Was she a perfect mother? Definitely not. But she tried her best. At least, she *thought* she did. She had to stop thinking about what might have been and focus on this incredible, caring, sensitive little person. Michele peeled off her ballet flats that now looked more grey than cream after her impromptu run, and stepped over to where Henry slept. She crouched down and swept a rogue section of hair from his eyes before kissing his forehead. *It really is just you and me against the world, kid,* she thought. *We don't need anyone else. We have each other.*

She stood up and circled around to her bed. *I really should have a shower.* She turned her head to the side and down to sniff her armpit. "Ew," she muttered, making a face. Staring at the bathroom door, she weighed her options. As amazing as the hot water and steam would feel right now, she couldn't take another step. That, and the pipes had a tendency to scream and pop and make all kinds of other disconcerting noises. She pulled back her sheet and blanket and slipped into bed, tunnelling down as far as she could as she covered herself. Her jeans and tank top felt uncomfortable against the sheets and it was too warm on this level of the house but tonight she didn't care. She wanted to feel the full weight of the bedding on her entire body right up to her chin for the few hours she had before it was time to get up again. She wanted to be like Mrs. Eliades' bread dough, soft and snug under layers of towels while ingredients worked inside to make it rise. At that moment the red digits on her bedside clock radio changed to 12:00. *It's a new day,* Michele noted before drifting off to sleep.

CHAPTER 2

If I did not know the cruelty of fate before, I know it now. To lose Philippe and then you, my love, was devastating. But rather than being left alone to mourn this great loss, I am forced to defend what you and I shared. I do not want to fight but at the same time I know what your wishes were. I must think of Edith's future. She is all that I have left.

I was surprised when you told me about the other part of your life that you left back in France, though perhaps I should not have been. I understood your reasons for walking away. You were a humble man, drawn to the simple life and happier to work with your hands than in business, but crossing an ocean did not cross your name from the ledger or the family.

They call me a seeker of gold. If you had not been taken from me so suddenly, we would have been united by the bonds of marriage. I do not want anything from them, but I must speak up because of my circumstances. I doubt that I will win against their resources, but I must fight or risk losing my home too.

* * *

Monday, August 10, 2009

She was running, but wasn't sure where. It was pitch black around her, yet Michele threw her body onward with shocking force. Something was chasing her, but that, too, was a mystery. "Where am I?" Her voice came out as a strange echo. *What is this place?* Spotting a single light in the distance, she started toward it and then all at once was there, as if time had skipped. She stood under a lamp post and squinted her eyes against the glare. She was a lone performer on a stage in a show she hadn't auditioned for; she did not have a script, didn't know her part. Droplets of perspiration crawled down her forehead. With her hands cupped around her mouth like a megaphone, she yelled to the rows of seats below, "I'm sorry! I'm not supposed to be here," and waited. The light obscured her view so she could not tell if there was even an audience at all. "Hello?" She edged herself to the front of the stage and tried to make out whether or not there was anyone there.

A whirring noise, followed by the sound of pulleys and rope working together, made her jump. On the stage, a set had appeared: a park. Rutledge Park. Her eyes widened. "What is happening!" A large pink elephant on wheels rolled across the floor without being pushed or pulled. Even though she could hear mechanical clicks and squeaks, she couldn't determine the source. How was it possible that the elephant was moving? As she looked on, it rotated its lacquered pink head and blinked its painted black eyes at her before turning away. Michele's jaw fell. She took a step forward but was unsure if this was the best direction to go. Maybe it would be better to run again instead. Just then the red velvet curtain fell, blocking the park and the elephant. She scurried ahead and peered between the curtains, but everything on stage was gone. The house lights came up.

She spun around and now the seats were in clear view. All of them were empty except one. Henry sat alone in the middle of the centre row, arms crossed, frowning. What was he doing here? "Henry?" Michele cried out. He didn't move. "Henry!" She shrieked, her voice getting higher. He stood, gave her a hard stare, and made his way along the row to the aisle and then to the exit that was just out of her sight. Then the theatre crumbled into dust. She was outside once more, and the night sky had clouded over. She scoured the immediate area. "Henry, where are you? Come back!"

The weather was changing. She could feel a storm coming and she had to get Henry inside. *He shouldn't be out here alone.* A ripple of green on the ground caught her attention. Squatting, she saw it was a twenty-dollar bill, and then picked it up, rubbed the note between her fingers. Two steps ahead, another one fluttered in the strengthening breeze. She jammed them in her pocket as she followed the path of paper. When she pulled another one from the blades of grass, the skies broke open and a fat, warm drop fell on her head. More drops came in slow motion, clinging to strands of hair and gliding across her cheek like snails. *Ugh, why is this rain sticky?* She let go of the money and wiped her face with the back of her hand.

She opened her eyes and a long string of drool stretched down from an open canine mouth. Above it, the droopy red eyes of a bloodhound watched her. "Ugh, Ares!" Mrs. Eliades' dog towered over the low-rise bed. Michele flailed her arms and legs, trying to free herself from the sheets and blankets. Ares waited, unfazed by her reaction. She shot out of bed and nearly tripped on the bedding, her heart racing. She huffed and put her hands on her hips, staring the dog down.

"Seriously, Ares? That is *so* gross." She brushed her cheeks and hair off. It was going to be difficult to forget that wake-up call. A giggle from the other bed made her look up. Henry sat upright, eyes smiling and a hand over his mouth as he tried to stifle his amusement. "It's not funny!" Michele pointed at him. But Henry's reaction was infectious, and she felt herself giving in to it. Plus, half his hair was sticking straight out, his blankets were in a bundle, and one pyjama pant leg was pushed all the way up.

"Mummy, Ares says, 'Good morning!'" Hearing his favourite

little boy say his name, the canine bayed and trotted over to him, climbed onto the bed paw by paw, and snuggled him like a lap dog. Henry shrieked with delight and gave him a hug.

Michele chuckled and her laughter increased until she glanced at the clock radio. It was 8:00 a.m. "Oh no. No, no, no. I'm late!" She became aware of her clothes and remembered the outfit, the run, the dream. Her expression hardened. "Henry." His features came to life as she said his name. "Please get dressed. As fast as you can. You're going to help Didi today, and I've got to get ready for work. Quick, quick!" His whole demeanour wilted and Ares, ever sensitive, put his head on the boy's leg. Henry gave him a pat, slipped out from under him, and marched to his dresser. Michele grumbled on her way to the bathroom. Her carefully calculated schedule had already been disrupted, only a few minutes into the morning. It would be hard to recover from that. Organization and order were the only way to start the day, but with a child, these were elusive. She yearned for them to return to optimal levels.

She shut the door and turned the water on, letting it run as she peeled off her sweaty jeans, tank top, and underclothes. The pipes popped and creaked as they came to life and she pictured tiny gnomes working deep underground, turning cranks and pulling levers to pump the water up from the earth and through the pipes into the house. *That's silly. I've really got to wake up.* She shook the image away and waved her hands back and forth under the tap to test the temperature. The water was still cold, but Michele was going to have to go double-time to get caught up so she braced herself and got into the shower. The shock jolted her awake and focused her. As she washed, she compiled the day's checklist so far: shower (check!), get dressed, grab something to eat, get to the archives. *Wait, I forgot: wrangle Henry and get him set up with Mrs. Eliades for the day while avoiding unnecessary conversation. Right. No problem.* She finished up, turned off the still-cool water, and got out of the shower. After wrapping herself in a thin towel, she stomped into the bedroom. *Let's do this*, she told herself, shivering.

Fifteen minutes later, she raced downstairs. Her hair was still wet and she had minimal makeup on, but she was dressed and looked good enough to go to work. Luckily air-drying made her hair go wavy, and she could apply more lip gloss and blush on the bus ride. She rushed into the kitchen and found Henry at the table, Batman T-shirt on inside-out so that the bat signal's colour was inverted. He had pulled a box of Cheerios from the cupboard and the blue mixing bowl from the counter. A line of *o*'s led across the floor and onto the table, where he was picking out and eating the few that were left in the bowl.

"I made breakfast!" He sat up tall.

She surveyed the mess and rubbed her throbbing temples. *I do not have time for this.* She had to act fast. By her estimation, she had about ten minutes at most before she had to dash for the bus. Mrs. Eliades would appear any minute and Michele wanted to minimize the overlap. Precision was key. She scooped cereal into her hand, dumping it each time into the mixing bowl. One thing was for certain: Mrs. Eliades kept a spotless house. So, there was really no reason to waste food.

Just as Michele gathered the last of the *o*'s, the screen door squeaked and the back door opened. Sunlight pushed through the entryway, spilling across the checkered floor and pooling in the black and white squares. A familiar silhouette, short and broad, stood briefly in the doorway and as it advanced, Mrs. Eliades materialized. Michele's breath caught in her throat and she hoped Mrs. Eliades hadn't been able to hear it.

"Ah, Michele, good morning, good morning. Is beautiful day again." Mrs. Eliades pointed at the sun with her chin, a sunflower following the light. Her cheeks were rosy and her eyes half-closed, and standing there she looked for a split-second like the young girl she had been in Greece. Henry must have noticed and recognized a kindred spirit because he jumped off his chair and ran over to her, beaming. Mrs. Eliades grabbed his face. "And here is the handsome boy! You have a hug for Didi this morning? Oh yes! You a good boy. Henry, you hungry? Didi will make you something." He started to tell her about the cereal but Michele jumped in, worried Mrs. Eliades might realize he'd used her favourite mixing bowl.

"Henry ate a little bit, but I'm sure he wouldn't say no to some of your wonderful cooking," Michele complimented her. "That is," she said, remembering that Mrs. Eliades had already been working that morning, "if you're not too tired."

Mrs. Eliades dismissed the remark with her hand. "The boy needs to eat, I feed him. I clean early this morning, so I was already outside pulling some weeds. We have some jobs in the garden today for me and my wonderful helper!" She put her plump mouth to Henry's ear and whispered conspiratorially, "But first, we eat!"

Perfect, Michele thought. *They're all set so I can make my getaway.* "Well, have fun, you two. I've gotta run, er, go." After last night, she didn't want to think about running. She threw open the fridge, pulled an everything bagel from the bag, and took a bite. Her backpack was in the front hall, so she chewed on her way out of the kitchen. She wasn't fast enough. Quick footsteps followed behind her and then Mrs. Eliades' big voice boomed.

"Michele, I hope you no forget that I need to talk with you today. Is important. Maybe you forget because was late yesterday, so I want to make sure you know. You have a few minutes now?" Mrs.

Eliades had cornered her at the parson's table.

Michele faced her, but leaned away. "I'm so sorry, but I have to get to work. I'm a bit late and need to make the next bus." She shuffled along the table, the wooden edge digging into her back. "We'll talk … later." Mrs. Eliades raised her finger and opened her mouth to speak, but Michele grabbed her bag and spun out the door, pulling it after her. "Bye!" *I can't keep avoiding her forever*, she told herself as she flew down the stairs. *But I'm going to have to try for as long as I can.* She hurried to the corner, crossed Alder Street, and turned left onto Cloverdale. Douglas Street was only a few blocks away, but it was a decent distance when you were in a time crunch. The events of last night, the crazy dream, and her muddled thoughts from this morning all turned in her head. She did not want to run, but at this point she didn't have a choice.

* * *

An electronic sign on a nearby business displayed the time; she had made it with minutes to spare. Her shoulders relaxed and she took in the government building for a moment. She still felt like she had to pinch herself every time she arrived at work. It was a part-time job, but it was a city job with benefits. That was huge. Most importantly, it was archives. It was history. After a year of volunteering there between her odd jobs, a position had opened up. She hadn't had any experience, but in that year of filing and sorting news articles and then photographs, Michele had learned a lot. She'd taken on anything and everything that had been asked of her and then begged for more. In her heart she had known she'd found her dream career; she just needed to convince the archivist to hire her. Maybe Janice had noticed how keen she was, or maybe it had been a case of being in the right place at the right time. Either way, Janice had chosen her, and Michele was going to hold onto this job for as long as possible.

She floated into the archives and let the sweet, musky smell envelope her. Cases of reference and local history books lined the wall to her right. Some were new, written by historians who had come to the archives for source material. Some, kept in their own locked case, were much older: one-hundred-year-old provincial agricultural reports, books by Nellie McClung, an early history of the Women's Institute. On the opposite wall, rows of cabinets held the vertical files she knew so well, arranged by subject or last name. She weaved her way through the tables, straightening the signs that laid out the requirements for researchers. The rules were engraved in her brain just as much as on the signs. Pencils only. One file at a time. No food or drinks. No licking fingers to turn pages, (it was amazing to her that people had to be told this, but they did). Some visitors scoffed when she explained all of this to them. Clearly, they didn't feel the awe of holding history in their hands. It was a powerful feeling, and as the saying went, with great power came great responsibility. And in the case of archives, many rules.

As she approached the reception desk, the red and green covers of the city directories drew her eye. Next to the vertical files, they were her favourite resource to work with. Within their pages she could time travel through the entire life of a house, from its construction as someone's brand new home, to children growing up and getting jobs, to a widow left alone within its walls, to its last breath when it was torn down to make way for a Texaco service station. In the same way, the directories traced neighbourhoods. Michele could look up a street and find out when it had first appeared by that name, what it had been called previously, and how many buildings sat along its sides. Most interestingly, she could learn how it had developed and changed with each passing year. And of course, the directories had something to say about families, too. Where they had lived. How they had made their living through the course of their lives here. Who they had loved.

Tucking her backpack under the desk, she fired up her computer. Janice, already in her office in the back room, popped her head out and gave her a brusque wave before retreating again. *Hmm, she must be busy with something this morning.* Shrugging, Michele sat down and opened the email program. *Ooh, I hope I have some fun inquiries today.* After the messages had downloaded, she deleted the spam, flagged the administrative emails for Janice, and then skipped straight to those that, from their subject lines, looked like questions from the public. "OK, no better place to start than with the first one," she told herself, clicking.

She read:

Hello, my name is Daphne Williams and I live in Grand Forks. I am trying to find out about my grandparents. I know that they lived in Victoria in the 1940s, but I don't have any other information. I would like to know which house they lived in so I can see it when I come out to visit next month. I've been told that my grandfather had a shoe repair business, so I would like to find that as well if possible. Finally, I'm hoping that you can provide information on where and when they got married, when they died, and grave location. I've set aside time to drive around to these places during my visit, provided that I can figure out where they are. I've included my grandparents' full names below. Thank you in advance for your help.

Michele reread the message twice, practically drooling. This inquiry was the archives equivalent of being presented with a gourmet meal. It looked good, it activated all her senses, and she couldn't wait to dig in. Technically she should probably direct Daphne to hire her own researcher to do this level of work, since the question was not a straightforward reference request, but Janice was occupied and wouldn't notice, and besides, no one had come in yet. Michele could take this deep dive into Daphne's family without drawing attention to it. If a researcher walked in, she would take a break, that was all. In the meantime, she would enjoy the records, savouring each bite as she found every last morsel of information they might contain on Daphne Williams' grandparents. Michele would not be satisfied until she'd consumed everything. If the answers were there, she would find them.

The finding aids were the place to start. She pulled up the file list on the computer and scrolled through the names. They seemed endless. But each entry represented someone's story. A story that she had the privilege of sharing for the present and safeguarding for the future. When she spoke with people about her job, they would inevitably ask her to check if there was a file on their family. If that family had indeed lived in the area and not a neighbouring town with its own archives, then she would make a note of the name, look it up the next time she was at the archives, and report back. Even Amanda had been curious, but Michele hadn't found much for her. Sometimes the answers just weren't there. So, Amanda had taken a chance and encouraged Michele instead: "Hey, you should look up your last name! Maybe there will be something about your family in there." But just as with John and Barbara, she had turned down the suggestion. That was the one inquiry she wouldn't take on.

In her time with the archives, Michele had never once been

tempted to look. The reason was simple: she did not have questions, so she did not need answers. In her case, it was just biology, and she wasn't interested in DNA. Why waste any energy on it? She continued to scroll up and down through the list of names. These were the families that needed her. She could explore their trees, following the long branches to generations of descendants. She could give them names and faces and a voice. She wanted—needed—to know all of them. She followed them from birth to death and the phases in-between. With them, it was different. It was all about the details. She got to know them and, in some cases, like with the Tolmie family, became more personally invested because they had heard the same gravel crunching under their feet, admired the same undulating landscapes, travelled the same routes across town (though at much different speeds), as she did. Through research, organization, and a little imagination, she could connect with them and take comfort in the commonalities.

Which was why she needed to help Daphne find her grandparents. Michele examined the finding aid, slowing down when she got to the right letter. W, Wi... Williams. A common last name, so there were a lot of files. *Hmm, let's see.* She took a closer look at the Williams entries until she hit pay dirt. Score! According to the list, there was a file that could be for the person she was looking for. Her hand jumped from the computer mouse, anxious to touch documents rather than electronics. She charged to the filing cabinets, zeroed in on the drawer marked V-Z, and pulled it open. Her fingers danced across the tabs until she came to the file. After setting it on a table, she flipped it open and it was like lifting the lid of a treasure chest, contents shining brilliantly and projecting a golden display onto her face. Michele skimmed the documents and was sure this was the right person. It wasn't a thick file, but the records inside provided enough breadcrumbs to lay down a trail for her to follow.

Her body struggled to catch up with her brain as she went to the city directories. The thrill of the hunt, of finding the next clue, brought a welcome surge of endorphins. She shifted a 1949 edition forward from the shelf, careful not to put pressure on the damaged spine. At the table she opened the book and navigated to W. Endless pages of Williams did not deter her. Michele ran her finger down each one until she found the correct first initial. She reached over to the reference desk, grabbed a pencil and a scrap piece of paper, and jotted down possible matches and their addresses. Then she turned to the other half of the directory where listings were organized by street. One by one she looked up each of the addresses she'd written down and there, she located the next lead: first names. She pulled the file closer and cross referenced the information she had found on Daphne's grandparents with that in the directory. The pencil hopped and skipped across the paper with every notation. For thirty minutes, Michele worked her way back through the 1940s and 1930s until there it was. She had found them, there in black and white.

After that, it was a matter of taking the details she'd gathered and going online to some genealogy and vital statistics websites to find the marriage, death, and burial information. She wrote up a detailed summary and emailed it to Daphne. Michele had never met her and might not ever meet her. She might not even get a response. Sometimes she would spend an hour researching for someone and send off the information, never to hear from them again. But she never forgot an inquiry, the person it came from, or the ancestors it led her to. As she reread her findings, she envisioned Daphne seeing them for the first time, sitting down in surprise and joy, perhaps getting teary-eyed. Michele hoped Daphne would be just as thrilled with the results as she had been to uncover them.

Over the next few hours, she went through the rest of the emails, researching and responding to all of the questions that had landed in the archive's inbox. Some were really easy, like looking up the origin of a street name. Some were a bit more involved, though not as time-consuming as the Williams inquiry had been. And for a couple of them, she couldn't find the answer to the exact question that had been posed, but in her search had turned up some tidbits she believed might be relevant. She never wanted to send anyone away empty-handed, so she always tried to provide some piece of information they could squirrel away for future reference. You never knew when it could be useful later on. Satisfied she'd done her best, she got up and stretched her neck and shoulders. When she was in the zone, she lost all track of time. She would forget to eat, to go to the bathroom, to blink. Especially if no one came into the archives, which had been the case today. Come to think of it, she hadn't even spoken with Janice. Michele wondered what was keeping her so occupied.

Curious, she approached the back room. As if reading her mind, Janice emerged, looking drawn. "Hey, Michele. Sorry to leave you on your own out here today. I hope you weren't too swamped?"

"No one came in, but it was steady with email inquiries," Michele replied. "I got through all of them, though. All good. Actually, it was a lot of fun—as always." She grinned.

Janice turned her wrist to check the time on her slim watch and held onto the tan leather band with her other hand. "We've got another fifteen minutes or so before it's time to close up. I'm wondering if we could sit down and chat about something. It partially relates to inquiries." She looked Michele in the eye. It was obvious something was bothering her, but she gave nothing away. She extended her arm, directing them to the nearest table.

Once they had sat down on opposite sides, Michele asked,

"What's up?"

Hands clasped in front of her, Janice spoke. "I've been on the phone all day—as you may have noticed—with administration, finance, human resources, the union. I'm afraid there may be imminent changes coming that will impact the archives."

Michele felt her heart sink heavy down her chest and into her gut like a rock tossed into water and falling to the ocean floor. "Oh?"

"Since the crash last year, the powers-that-be have been reviewing all of the positions and taking a closer look at the budget. Today they came back with their list of proposed cutbacks in what they view as 'expendable areas.'" Janice's expression was sympathetic as she continued. "Unfortunately, as in so many organizations, they don't fully understand the importance of archives. And even though our numbers have been going up, and I really need someone to help me out here, they want to reduce the hours for your position. I've been arguing with them, explaining what an asset you are, but this is bureaucracy at its worst. Their plan is to implement this for the fall."

"Oh, um, wow. This seems really sudden." Michele reeled as she processed the implications.

Janice leaned forward and opened her hands, laying them palm-up on the table. "I know. But the review has been going on for a while now behind the scenes. I was hoping that if we kept our heads down and carried on, they would pass us over. And there's more, I'm afraid."

"More?"

"Management is no longer allowing any extra time without pre-approval from a director, which means our requests would go to my boss." She rolled her eyes. "I've been told there are absolutely no additional hours, including banked time, until further notice. On top of that, they want us to prioritize more quantifiable projects. Governments love numbers. So, we have to slash our inquiry response time. If someone has a more involved question, we'll have to direct them to a freelance researcher. But don't worry," she tried to reassure Michele. "I'm not giving up on your position yet. I will do what I can to keep you at the same hours. If anything, I would love if they gave you more. There's such a backlog of processing to do, and I'm hoping that we can start to tackle that."

Michele felt tears begin to sprout from the corners of her eyes but stomped them back with the heel of her hand. She would be mortified to break down in front of her mentor, the person who had given her a chance. "Thanks, Janice. I would really like to be able to work on that. Thanks for fighting for me."

"Hey, it's archives. We need to stand up for them. We don't always win, but we have to try." Janice smiled. "Why don't you take off. I can lock up."

With a nod Michele pushed her chair out and went behind the reception desk for her backpack. She scampered out of the building like a wounded deer and darted for cover under the bus shelter. With her eyes cast down, the tears returned in a torrent until they were all she could see on the cement under her.

* * *

An hour later, she dragged herself up the front steps of the house. Her eyes were confused maps, red lines crossing the white surface like a poor example of urban planning. She had used her lip gloss and blush to try to hide the evidence. *Fake it 'till you make it,* she had recited. Maybe Janice would be able to sort everything out at the archives. Hadn't she basically said that nothing was final yet? Michele had to continue like it would all be OK, even if she did not know how. Even if she didn't truly believe it herself. She unlocked the front door and dumped her backpack on the floor just inside. Upstairs, Henry played with his toy ambulance. The "*nee-noo, nee-noo*" sounds he made with his young voice tumbled down the steps to her ears. But her mind, already fragile, filtered him out. All she could hear were sirens.

In the living room, Mrs. Eliades waited in the armchair with her hands holding onto opposite elbows. Michele froze in place, then hobbled towards her. The news about her job had unsettled her so much that she'd forgotten to strategize her arrival. Her days of successful evasion were clearly coming to an end. The moment for real talk had arrived. Just like Janice had done, Mrs. Eliades gestured for Michele to sit. The couch, which had always sagged in the middle since Michele had moved in, had never felt so stiff.

"Michele," Mrs. Eliades stated. "We talk now."

"Yes, of course." Michele gulped.

Mrs. Eliades wasted no time. "Michele, you live in my house quite a few years now. You a good tenant, you quiet, you clean."

"Um, thank you—"

"Wait, I no finish. You like it here, yes?"

"Yes! Very much."

"OK, but in these months, you know, you always pay the rent late. And now, is even more late."

Michele hung her head. "I know, and I'm so sorry. I promise—"

Mrs. Eliades cut her off. "You know that more bills come today? On *coloured* paper. Those are the bad ones."

"I'll get the money soon—"

"I like you, Michele. I hope you know. Because I help you a lot. So many times I pay for you, I give you more time. But now is too long."

Michele looked at the parson's table and saw a new heap of

envelopes beside the one she had knocked over yesterday, the latter now magically back in its place. She hadn't noticed the additions on her way in, but then again, she had been distracted. "I'll make it up to you, really. Just give me a chance," she begged.

Mrs. Eliades looked sad but resolute. "I can't give you no more chances. If this happens again in September, then you have to move out. I'm sorry. I no can afford more breaks for you, Michele."

Michele debated what to say next but she couldn't come up with anything adequate. She was empty. Maybe she should retreat and regroup; anything to get away from the awkwardness. But while she thought, Henry came pummelling down the stairs, racing his ambulance along the banister. He bounced to her and drove the vehicle along her legs before he made it take a jump to the dark brown velour of the couch. He pushed it along the bumpy cushions and up the arm, then sent it flying across the crevasse to the armchair. Mrs. Eliades, indulging him, urged Henry to follow the contours of the chair up and over the back and around the armrest to her lap.

"My boy, you a crazy driver!" she teased, reaching out to give him a tickle but then letting him get away.

"No, Didi, I have to go! Someone needs help. Nee-noo nee-noo," he wailed. Once again he made the ambulance take off through the space between Mrs. Eliades and Michele. She was only half paying attention, so she flinched when his hand brought it down hard on her thigh. It was the same spot she'd bruised herself against the table in the dark the night before. "Watch out, Mummy, it's an emergency!" he warned.

It sure is, kid. It sure is.

CHAPTER 3

You are gone. We celebrated Christmas, with all of its promises of hope, and then everything was taken away. Our hopes, our plans, and our joys all vanished forever on December 26 when your heart, always so full of love, stopped beating. You had mended mine, but now it has been shattered again, and there will be no repairing it. This was to have been such a joyous season for us—bringing in a new year and celebrating second chances; setting a date for our wedding; being a family, just the three of us.

Instead I have sealed myself inside. My house has become a tomb, which is only fitting since you are buried in your own. I am lost without you. I stay in bed all day, but do not sleep. I do not eat. A few women have called in with a cassoulet or a beef bourguignon. I have refused to see anyone, but I am grateful for the food and company for Edith. She occupies herself with the doll you gave her, setting her in the wooden chair made by your own hand. She will make a good mother one day. If only you would be here to see it with me in our old age.

* * *

Tuesday, August 11, 2009

That morning there had been no sneaking around or avoiding. Now that Mrs. Eliades had laid out her position, Michele no longer needed to hide. And Mrs. Eliades was the type of person who did not like to explain herself more than once. Those who forced her to were likely to be added to her blacklist, and that wasn't a good place to be. She had set her terms the night before, and there would be no changing her mind; they might as well have been written on a stone tablet. Now it was up to Michele to adhere to them or find somewhere else to live. Mrs. Eliades hadn't said a word about the matter at breakfast and had carried on as usual, tousling Henry's bed-head and serving him a meal of fresh olive bread, cheese, yogurt, and some leftover chicken—cubed to be easily eaten. Michele had opted for her everything bagel, but this time made the effort of smearing both halves with cream cheese before she walked out with it in hand. For all intents and purposes it was a regular day, but appearances were deceiving. Mrs. Eliades had made direct eye contact a few times and there was no mistaking the message: pay up or get out.

Michele had arrived at work ten minutes early and was sitting on the bench outside the building, staring at the archives sign beside the entrance. Not only could she lose her home, but now she could lose her burgeoning career, too. This job was her life. She was good at it. They couldn't just start chipping away at it hour by hour, discarding her labour as if it was unskilled. As if any warm body could fill in, because what did they even do in archives anyway? It wasn't right. And researching was the best part. It was at the heart of archives. Now they wanted to take that away, too? As she focused on the blank exterior wall, her mind set up a slide show of her memories at the archives. With each blink, the projector carousel turned and advanced the slide: she saw the first inquiry she had handled without any direction from Janice, ("What stood on that spot on Oak Street before the car dealership was built?"); the first time she'd held an original document, (the city's incorporation papers); the first glowing response she had received from a member of the public, ("We are so grateful for all the work that you did to find the answer for us."). And every day since those "firsts" had been better than the last. She wouldn't let them go easily. *I'll show those bureaucrats how valuable I can be.*

She got up from the bench and strutted into the archives, head held high. *You're going to keep doing what you do best, you got that?* She had geared herself up to work on more inquiries, but found Janice sitting out at the reference desk. In response to Michele's quizzical look, she stood up and smiled.

"Good morning! I know that yesterday was a bit rough for you, and I just want you to know that I meant what I said. I'm going to keep working on it. I was also serious about trying to get that backlog down. So, I have a plan for the next few weeks, starting today."

"OK." Michele perked up.

"Right." Janice got to it. "So, since it's generally quieter in August, I'm going to sit out here and look after things. I'll help any researchers, though I don't expect many, and respond to emails. In between, I'm going to keep making calls and trying to figure out how to fend off the cutbacks, or at least find some kind of work-around."

"Alright, so what am I going to be doing?"

"You'll be in the vault, getting more familiar with the records in there," Janice explained.

Michele raised her eyebrows, surprised. "Oh! OK, that sounds good." She reached around Janice, ditched her backpack under the desk, and pushed her elbow-length sleeves up her arms. "Tell me what to do, and I'll get started!"

Janice sat back down at the desk and double-clicked on a file. "I'll print off our vault inventory for you. It hasn't been updated in years, which is not great. Before I get you going on some backlog processing, it would be really useful to make sure we know exactly what we have. Your job is to go through every shelf and cross reference it with this list. Check off every collection and make a note if the location has changed since this was done last time. Also, record anything that isn't listed; we'll need to accession those." She grimaced. "Things weren't always done consistently back in the early years." Janice went to the commercial-sized printer and pulled out the sheets of paper that had come through, still warm, and gave them to Michele. "Let me know if you have any questions. And remember, the powers-that-be like numbers. This is a perfect project to show them. It has to be our focus."

"I'm on it." Michele snatched a pencil from the reference desk before going into the vault. As she entered, she felt the sharp temperature change against the bare skin of her forearms. She knew Janice kept a sweater back there because it got chilly when working in the space for long periods, but on a warm summer day it was the best place to be in the building. It was cool and a welcome change from the heat outside.

She walked through the windowless room, surveying each aisle to get an idea of the task ahead. Grey archival boxes packed every shelf of the powder-coated steel units. Map cabinets lined the wall by the door except for the far corner, where a utility table hid under boxes and bundles and files of donated and transferred records waiting to be seen and heard again. They attracted her as if they had a strong magnetic pull and she were a malleable sheet of metal. *I bet there's a lot of great stuff in there* ... She struggled but succeeded in forcing herself away. That inventory wasn't going to get done on its own.

The first unit directly opposite the table was the best place to begin. Michele worked her way through it, systematically consulting the list and checking boxes. When she had returned the last box back from the unit to its slot on the bottom shelf, she stretched, interlacing her fingers and pulling her arms towards the ceiling. As she twisted her body from side to side, her gaze went back to the backlog. Her fingers tingled. *You know, I could take a couple of minutes before starting the next unit. The health and safety office is always reminding us to get up and move every hour, and to focus on something else once in a while to give our eyes a break. Besides, if I'm going to be working on this backlog after the inventory, it would be good to have an idea of what I'll be dealing with.*

Michele brought her arms down and stepped to the table. She opened a box and skimmed through the pages, finding minutes, reports, and financial statements. Disappointed, she closed the box and moved on to a loose file. It contained six black and white family photographs with scalloped edges, along with a gift form. *Ooh, these look interesting.* She replaced the file without touching the photos—she didn't have gloves on—and reached over the table for a bunch of letters. But the table was too deep, she was too short, and she didn't want to lean on the other, closer records for fear of damaging them. If she could just get a bit of space to move. She gripped the table and shimmied it forward. Then she heard the slap of something falling to the floor.

Panicked, she crawled underneath the table. She hadn't seen anything so close to the back edge that it would fall. However, contrasted against the cold, white floor lay what appeared to be an album. *What is this?* She looked over her shoulder, even though she was the only one in the vault, and then picked it up. It had a textured dark brown cover, bound with a matching cord that could have been a shoelace. Embossed gold lettering on the front read, "Diary." Holding it in one hand and using her other hand for support, she backed herself out from under the table and got to her feet. She needed an empty surface; a map cabinet would do. She moved over and set the diary on top. The cabinet was tall, so Michele had to stand on her tiptoes to be able to see. She walked her fingers across the terrain of the front cover like a divining rod waiting for a twitch.

A current of uncertainty jumped through her. *Maybe I shouldn't be doing this, after all. Remember what Janice said: focus. But I've come this far.* She reverently opened the diary, certain it had something to say. Everything in her body screamed that she had to find out what that was.

The first page of writing told her two things: the entries began in 1938, and they were written in French. *French? Really?* She did an initial pass through the pages, turning them one by one until she reached the end. Yes, the whole thing was in French. "You've got to be kidding me," she mumbled. It wasn't that she didn't know French. John and Barbara had enrolled Amanda and Michele in late-entry Immersion in middle school. Amanda had struggled all the way through high school, but Michele, even though she hadn't been keen on it, had been a natural. It had driven Amanda crazy. She had worked twice as hard just to keep up, while Michele had hardly put any effort in and yet excelled. It had just seemed easy. She couldn't explain it. Madame Laurier had tried to encourage her to continue with language studies after graduation, singing in the cadence of her Parisian French, "*Mais vous avez un don inné pour le français.* You have a gift for it." Michele had shrugged, responding with perfect vocabulary and pronunciation, "I do not think that I am going to use French. At this point, I do not really know *what* I want to do with my life." Which had been true, until she'd discovered archives.

Michele pushed her toes harder into the floor to give her an extra sliver of height. She went back through the diary in reverse order. There was no gift form tucked between the pages. She lowered her feet back down and wiggled her cramped toes. Leaving the diary on the map cabinet, she returned to the processing table and looked for a matching form. Perhaps it had been separated by mistake. Maybe it had been put with another donation? She checked the boxes and the files. Everything seemed to be where it belonged. All the records had a corresponding gift or transfer form. There was definitely a significant backlog of material to process, but all of the records were in order and documented. She could see the donor information, brief descriptions, custodial history. She knew where they came from. The diary was the only orphan.

Someone had poured years of themselves letter by neat letter into this book, what, seventy years ago, and now those words were forgotten behind a table, anonymous? It was tragic. It wasn't unheard of for one-off, "mystery" items to turn up in an archives, but these were the exception rather than the rule—ideally, at least. She went back to the diary and turned it over in her hands, as if to conjure answers from it. She could swear she felt an energy pulsing from its centre, with circles radiating outwards like so many ripples of sound crashing one after another into her eardrums and pulling her in closer each time. A siren song. But, she asked herself, feeling the weight of the book, why was this random find different to her than others she and Janice had come across? Michele's forehead creased, then released. *This is silly. It's not different. I'm a researcher at heart, and I know that. If there's a mystery, I want to solve it. That's all. So, I just need to do a bit of digging and find out what I can about this diary. Then I'll be able to move on to the next thing.*

She walked to the processing table and was about to put the diary back with the rest of the backlog when she heard the door sweep brush against the floor as Janice came into the vault. Without thinking, Michele put the diary behind her back as she spun towards her boss. "Oh, hi! Hi, Janice!" *Smooth, real smooth.*

"I'm sorry, I didn't mean to startle you. I just wanted to see how you were making out back here. Everything going alright with the inventory?"

Michele moved towards the shelving, where she had left the list what seemed like ages ago. Clutching the diary in her right hand, she picked up the inventory sheet with her left and pretended to give it a once-over, nodding. "Yes, everything is great. Really great. Excellent." *Stop talking!* She tried to heed her own warning.

"That's—great. How far did you get? I'm hoping for a decent pace on this."

Michele remembered she'd finished only the first unit. She could have easily had a few more shelves done if she hadn't gone down a rabbit hole. "You know, it did take me a while to get oriented at first, so I'm not as far along as I'd like to be. But," she added, "I'm really on a roll now."

Janice was still two map cabinet lengths away, holding the door open. She glanced into the Reference Room to make sure no one had come in before addressing Michele. "I'm sure you'll make up the delay. But unfortunately, it's not going to be today. I managed to get a face-to-face meeting with administration, so I'm going there now. Hopefully I'll make some progress with them, but I have a feeling it will take the rest of the afternoon. Which means, I'll need you to come back to the reference desk. Do you have something that you can work on out here?"

The diary burned in Michele's hand. Now she knew how Ben Gates felt. The temptation was real. "Actually, I found something really interesting while I was doing the inventory."

"Oh?"

"It's not accessioned, and there's no paperwork. I think it might have been in the vault for a long time. It's in French, so it's going to take some work to go through." She crumpled the edge of the inventory sheet. "I know you said we have to spend less time on research, but would it be OK if I started digging into it?"

Janice smiled. "Yes, of course. I get it. If I weren't heading out the door, I'd love to see it myself. But you'll have to limit yourself to when you're out front, in between other things."

Michele mentally counted the pages. "It's just that, I think it deserves more attention. There's a story there."

"You know I can't give you even an extra half hour right now, let alone enough for in-depth research. Speaking of which, I really need to get going."

"Wait. I mean, what if—what if I came in on my own time? Like, stayed late, or came in on my days off. I understand the management stuff, but if I'm not getting paid, would I be allowed to do that?"

"Hmm." Janice stopped. "Well, I guess technically, if you came in as a researcher, it wouldn't go against policy. I'd have to give you a key, but that's doable. Let's talk tomorrow."

Michele resisted the urge to jump up and down. "Thank you, so much. Really. You go ahead to your meeting. I'll be sure to lock everything up at the end of the day. And thanks again."

Janice smiled. "You're welcome. I know you'll be fine, but send me an email if anything comes up."

The vault door closed, and Michele realized she'd been holding her breath. Her arms shook; the inventory sheet vibrated until she set it on a shelf. She scrambled to the vault door, opened it just wide enough to get a clear view, and caught a glimpse of Janice's back before the front door closed. Michele emerged from the coolness of the storage area into the warm Reference Room and went to the desk. She put the diary down and eyed it as if she'd just come out of hypnosis. *Why did I hide this from Janice? What's wrong with me? What if Janice had said no?* Michele pictured herself as the heroine in her own *National Treasure* story, and shuddered. It was a lot easier to slip than she'd thought. The recognition both surprised and horrified her.

Instead of the quick look-through she had done in the vault, she sat down and examined the diary for clues. The first page after the cover was blank, but her heart leapt when she looked at the other side. There, in small script in the bottom left-hand corner, was a name: *Clotilde*. "Clotilde." Michele ran the name over her tongue, along the top of her mouth, through her lips. She tasted each letter. Just knowing the name of the diary writer was like taking the first bite of a delicious treat. However, that alone wouldn't satisfy the desire for more. With her rusty French, she read. She couldn't understand every word, and even after going over the first entry twice, she still lacked some key vocabulary. Without it, she knew she was missing the most revealing parts. Something about leaves and autumn, which made sense since it was dated September. Clotilde had mentioned the ocean, too. Michele wondered where the words had been written. Europe? Or the East Coast? Was there any chance they could have been composed in British Columbia, or even on Vancouver Island? There must be a local connection if the diary had ended up here.

Even though she didn't know everything the entry said, one thing was obvious: it spoke of love. Michele blushed. She felt like she was intruding on something very private. Presumably Clotilde, whoever she was, had never planned on anyone else reading her most intimate thoughts. Clearly she had fallen for someone, and it must have been quite intense. Her words seemed so poetic—unless that was just the way French speakers expressed themselves. Maybe they were just naturally more creative. Michele thought back to the books and art she had studied in French Immersion. It seemed to her that those authors and artists were tuned into a whole different plane of inspiration that made them more sensitive to and observant of the emotions and beauty around them. Certainly much more so than uptight North Americans. *I guess we have too much on our minds. The French, they know love. They're famous for it, after all.*

She moved on to the next entries, reading closely so as not to overlook any important details, then bounced back to the first. From what she could gather, Clotilde had met her sweetheart sometime *after* leaving her home in France. *Aha, another clue.* So, Clotilde *had* come from France. But to where? Michele could feel her eyes wanting to jump ahead like racehorses waiting for the starting gates to open, but she reined them in. *Slow down, slow down.* She stayed the course down the pages and found another name written in that same steady hand. Philippe. She reread the section. Her French slowly reawakened in her brain; it opened its eyes and sighed and moved at the edges of her memory, reinvigorating itself with each word after years of dormancy. She allowed it to shift and stretch and expand. After all this time, she actually needed the language back. She had never wanted it so badly.

She continued to immerse herself in the diary's depths. There were now two people to find, and one of them, Clotilde, was going to help her do it. Michele continued trying to translate the words, becoming frustrated with her limitations until she reached a passage she could decipher. It looked like Clotilde and Philippe had indeed gotten married. Michele's cheeks flushed. Even though she didn't have much to go on yet, she was starting to feel like she knew this young couple. They had tied the knot! She grabbed the top sheet of scrap paper from the pile on the desk and made notes. If she could just find enough hints, she might be able to put the story together. "What else have you got for me, Clotilde?" she whispered, turning a page. She noticed the date and stopped. 1940. She checked the entries that immediately followed, looking only at the dates. It dawned on her that the next few were all from the time of the Second World War. She shivered. Going back over the part about the wedding, she realized that the date was also 1940. Clotilde and Philippe had gotten married during the thick of it. How had the war impacted the newlyweds?

Focused, Michele carried on. She followed Clotilde's orderly handwriting to the words that stood out: fight, air. Airforce. Fly. There it was. She looked up, pensive. So, Philippe was a pilot. He married his love in—she peeked at the previous page—May, and then a month later joined the war effort. It was difficult to imagine what that must have been like. She returned to the diary until she found a name that could not be mistaken: Vancouver. Her heart hammered in her chest. A local connection. Philippe had been in Vancouver before going to Europe. It didn't say if that was where he had enlisted, but he'd definitely trained there. She could picture the scene: Philippe standing with his blue-grey duffel bag at Pacific Central Station, waiting to board a train for the long trip across the country. She wondered if Clotilde had been there to say goodbye. Michele returned to the text. It sounded like Philippe had left her to *go* to Vancouver, so they must have lived somewhere else. Somewhere close?

She jotted down more notes on her sheet of paper and then resumed reading. The next date was 1943. Here the occasion was obvious, and it made Michele smile. Parenthood. Philippe must have come home, on leave or maybe because he had been injured and sent back from overseas. Clotilde's uniform swirls and slants announced the arrival of a daughter, Edith. Michele's grin stretched deeper into her cheeks. She suddenly had the desire to send congratulations, even though it was sixty-six years too late. It was an irrational thing to want to do, but in archives it was easy to form a bond with people who were long gone. Already she could feel herself slipping into a relationship. In just a few pages, she'd followed Clotilde through some major milestones. Eager to find out what happened next, Michele leaned in closer. *"... yeux gris." That's interesting. Edith had grey eyes just like Philippe. Just like Henry. How's that for coincidence?* It didn't seem to be a common colour, as far as she had seen. Michele didn't know anything else about what Clotilde's family looked like, but at least now she could visualize their eyes.

She felt as if they were watching her now, father and daughter encouraging her onward. With a burst of extra motivation, she stepped into 1944. She fixed her attention on the phrase *"l'effort de guerre"*—war effort. Not surprisingly, Clotilde had written about her wartime experiences. Taking in the entire page at once, Michele's own eyes widened and set off a reverberation down her spine and out along her limbs. *Yes, yes, yes!* Her chair squeaked as its wheels painted short strokes on the patterned carpet in a wild display. She jumped back and forth between three names: Government Street, the *Colonist* newspaper, and Cordova Bay. There was nowhere else that these could refer to other than Victoria. Here, in her own city. Philippe had gone to Vancouver but Clotilde had soldiered on here with Edith, living her life and finding her own ways to contribute. Michele concentrated on the sentences, teasing out their meaning. Apple pie. Clotilde had served it at the Salvation Army on Government Street. Michele recorded every new piece of the puzzle on paper: advertisements from the *Colonist*, airplanes at Cordova Bay. She got closer to the action with every detail. The home front was her home now too, on the same streets she herself travelled.

Her joy was short lived. Like Clotilde, she was anxious for Philippe to return to his family. But the next entry, dated a few months later, shattered that idea. There had been a telegram. The phrase "*présumé mort*"—presumed dead—said it all. She brought her hands to her mouth and felt tears sting the corners of her eyes. *No! How could this have happened?* It wasn't fair. Clotilde and Philippe had just started their life together. They'd been happy, even through the war and despite all the uncertainty around them. Their poor daughter would have been far too young to remember her dad. Michele sat for a few minutes, channeling Clotilde's sorrow. She had become a single mom just like that, and everything had changed. They had that in common, even though the circumstances were completely different. They weren't related and there were decades between them, but Michele felt a new closeness to this mysterious woman. *I hope that somehow she was OK. Clotilde, please tell me you were OK.*

She squeezed her eyes shut and crossed her fingers, as if somehow that could change the course of the past. She rushed through the next entry, but then had to backtrack to be sure she understood. Over a year had passed since Clotilde had lost her husband, but—Michele pored over the text—it looked like she had come through the other side. She'd found a friend in someone named Maurice. Michele silently cheered. *I knew you could do it, Clotilde. You are a tough, strong, woman. You've got this! And now you don't have to do it alone.* She followed along and learned that Maurice had been a huge help to Clotilde, supporting her every step of the way through her grief and beyond to healing. It seemed like Edith had liked him too. Pleased, Michele peered up at the clock and was astonished to find her shift was nearly over. It would be time to close the archives soon—but not without squeezing in just one more entry.

This one was different; she could tell that right away. Softer somehow. Perhaps more vulnerable, but beautiful. Clotilde wrote of music. With her words she painted a picture across the page of evenings spent by the fireplace, the moving melodies of the violin filling the room as Maurice played for her and her daughter. After all the tragedy and loss, she had found love again, and it seemed to have been a harmonious match with perfect timing. Michele hung this Norman Rockwell-style portrait, a living tableau of simple family life, above the mantle in her mind's eye so she could return to the scene again later. Finally, a happy ending! If only Clotilde had stopped there. Michele advanced the pages and counted four more entries. She glanced at the clock again and confirmed it was time to wrap up. It was a great spot to end for the day, but she regretted not being able to read the entire diary. The story wasn't over. Had the violin kept singing its sensuous ballad every evening at dusk? She assumed Clotilde and Maurice had married and remained in Victoria with Edith, spending the rest of their days together. The best possible outcome.

Michele lifted herself out of the chair, picked up the diary, and started towards the vault to put it back on the processing table. But halfway there, she slowed. Although she had to get home to relieve Mrs. Eliades, a thought had occurred to her. Michele wanted to take the diary with her to get a head start on the work, and she realized there was a way …

With a detour to lock the front door, she walked the precious book to the photocopier. Having assured herself of the flexibility and quality of the bindings, she slipped it onto the scan bed. *Turn page, press start, turn page, press start.* When the duplicate was complete, she bent down to unzip her backpack and placed the stack of loose sheets inside before returning the original to the vault. Now she could consult her old Le Robert and Collins French-English dictionary at home, and get a leg-up on the research while the diary remained safely in the archive.

Michele closed her bag and put her arms through the straps as smoothly as possible. It may have contained only copies, but it was still precious cargo. After turning off the lights and securing the vault, she crossed the threshold and pulled the locked door behind her. This was the start of something. She could feel it. And even though she questioned how one item could so quickly have taken over her life, it felt like she had to persevere until she uncovered the whole story, regardless of whether or not the reasons were clear. The diary was the city's property—something that belonged, by extension, to all the residents of the community. But at the moment, before it was accessioned and described and publicized, it was as if it belonged only to her. Staring ahead, Michele put one foot in front of the other and went directly to the bus stop.

It took every bit of her will power to not dig into her bag during the ride home. Instead, she tried to distract herself with her surroundings. A twenty-something blonde woman in the row ahead read Elizabeth Barrett Browning while winding a lock of hair around the index finger of her left hand. An elderly gentleman sat straight-backed across the aisle gripping two plastic bags of groceries. Behind him, a dark-haired man about her age wore a serious expression and a uniform; he was obviously on his way from the naval base at Esquimalt. Michele thought again of Philippe in his airforce blues, leaving the Island for the last time. She squirmed in her seat and used the action as an excuse to glimpse behind her. A middle-aged couple chatted and smiled as their pre-schooler bounced across their laps. The child pressed her chubby fingers against the dirty window to watch the bright colours of the fast food restaurants and boutique shop awnings flash by. Everywhere there were reminders of Clotilde and her family. Michele swivelled forward and rested the backpack at her feet. The copied pages vibrated inside.

By the time she called out her quick "thank you" to the driver, she was more than ready to burst out through the exit doors. She considered jumping down and skipping the steps altogether but changed her mind because the pages might crumple. She needed to be able to make out every word. Her walk to Alder Street was agonizingly slow and steady. *Careful, careful,* she repeated to herself until she reached her own steps. She glided up and unlocked the door, all the while strategizing how best to maximize her research time this evening. Inside, Henry was sprawled across the living room floor, a city of LEGO buildings and Hot Wheels cars surrounding him. An army of superhero action figures were lined up along the couch above, looking on. It was like watching a strange version of Gulliver and the Lilliputians. In the kitchen, Mrs. Eliades prepared dinner. Michele heard the clang of pots and pans and caught the spicy scent of oregano in her nose. Henry waved to get her attention and described the intricacies of the world he had created. She only half-listened, wondering how quickly she could get him to clean it up.

For the next few hours she went through the motions, picking up toys, eating dinner, getting Henry washed up and into bed. She had barely registered the zesty flavours of Mrs. Eliades' lemon chicken, a favourite dish. Ares, usually planted beside Henry's chair during meals, had laid himself at Michele's feet and followed her upstairs afterwards. After observing her rushed version of *Goodnight Moon* and short tuck-in, the dog, instead of inserting himself beside Henry, curled up at the end of her bed. She was too distracted to shoo him away. Using both hands, she pulled the weighty dictionary, blue dustcover worn at the corners, from the shelf in her night table and let it fall onto the blanket. Then she sat on the bed and pulled her backpack close enough to zip open. Finally, she brought out its contents. It was still light out, but she reached one arm under her pillow and fished out the small black emergency flashlight she kept there. She figured she would need it eventually; it could be a long night.

With her legs tucked up underneath her, she turned to the first page. She started at the beginning, hopping to the French-English dictionary every time she came to a word she'd skipped over. Despite her earlier language lapses, she had actually been fairly accurate in her initial translation. The emotions she had experienced the first time around came flooding back as she again travelled through Clotilde's life. Michele thought maybe they were even stronger now than before. On the other side of the room, Henry slept soundly. The rustling of pages floated like leaves through the room in a soothing lullaby. To her, it was a call to carry on. It did not take as long as she'd anticipated to get to the point where she had left off at the archives.

She deepened her concentration and read the final four entries. The rest of the story at last. Yes, she confirmed, Maurice and Clotilde were still together. Not married, it seemed, but committed to each other. Clotilde had written with so much hope about his promise to her. About how he wanted to look after her and her daughter. To provide for them for the rest of their lives. Michele paused and looked up. She traced the dark grooves in Ares' face as she pondered how exactly Maurice had made his living. She went to the next page, dated 1950—four years since the previous entry. Surely, they must have been married by then. Michele read the first sentence and her blood ran cold—"*Tu n'es plus.*" You are gone.—*This can't be. Not after Philippe. Not again.* She did not need the dictionary in order to finish. She could understand everything now but couldn't believe it. Maurice had died suddenly before he could marry Clotilde. Michele stared at the words in utter shock and then leaned back against her pillow, a tear falling down to meet it. Maurice had been wealthy, extremely so. He had chosen to walk away, entrusting the business to his family in France. But because he had technically not left behind a wife, that same family had refused to give Clotilde anything. *The end.* Michele wept as the last red rays from the sunset outside trickled down below the horizon.

CHAPTER 4

For the first time, I do not worry. Not anymore. You have claimed us as your own, and for this I am grateful. Philippe will always remain in my memory, and I will recognize him every day in Edith. I will look deeply into her grey eyes and will see his watching us from heaven. But you can be at ease because he would approve of you, I know it. He would appreciate your calm, quiet ways, maybe even more so because those qualities often eluded him. I was attracted to his carefree nature then, but you are what I need now. And now that the war is ended and life is starting to settle, we can, one step at a time, look to a future together. We are not rushed—the days stretch beautifully in front of us. Eventually we will make it official. Until that day, your word, your commitment is enough. You have made a promise to always provide for us, now and in the future. I do not want you to preoccupy yourself with money, but you assure me that you have some invested in the family business in France. It is comforting to know, but Edith and I will be fine as long as we have you.

* * *

Wednesday, August 12, 2009

The injustice! It was all Michele could think about on the ride to work the next morning. Sometime during the night, her sorrow had given way to anger. After everything, *everything*, that Clotilde had been through—marriage, war, motherhood, widowhood, new love, lost love—she and her daughter had been robbed of the only thing they had left: security.

The bus rocked as it drove over a patch of recent road work and Michele hugged her backpack to her chest. The diary pages were out of reach, but the pulse of the words moved through the fabric and up to the surface. Every heartbeat was a call to action as it hit her palms. Maurice's intentions had been clear: he had definitely wanted his money to go to Clotilde and Edith. And it seemed like his "family business" had been a lot more prosperous than he had let on; there was no way that it could have been just a small shop like Michele had originally thought. Clotilde had said something about not being able to fight Maurice's family. *They were obviously wealthy, but so greedy that they wouldn't respect his wishes.* Michele felt a growl, low and rumbling, develop at the base of her throat but it was lost under the engine noise.

So Clotilde had been left with nothing. Except, of course, for late nights of worrying about how to pay bills, put food on the table, buy school supplies for a young child. Michele sympathized, probably better than most given her own current financial situation. It was a terrible feeling to begin and end each day with that uncertainty and fear. And in Clotilde's case, at least, it had been entirely avoidable. Maurice's family could have afforded to give her some support. By choosing not to, they had not only cheated her out of money that should have been hers, they had done the same to Edith too. Who cared if Clotilde and Maurice hadn't been married? Hadn't their relationship counted for anything? Didn't love matter? Theirs had been the real deal. So many people never got the chance to experience it at all. Michele stared out the window as the bus stopped to drop off passengers. At the corner, a perky brunette with a long ponytail circled her slender arms around the neck of a man wearing a plaid shirt and ripped jeans. The couple kissed and then interlaced their fingers, sharing some private joke as they walked up the street. Michele turned away. Some people were lucky, and some weren't.

She sat in a daze until the bus reached her stop and the driver's rapid braking roused her. In the few minutes it took to walk to the archives, she made a decision. It would involve a lot of research but that was a bonus. She resolved to find them, all of them—Clotilde, Edith, Maurice, his family—and to make it right. Based on her math, Clotilde had likely already died, a fact on which Michele did not like to dwell, but there was a good chance Edith was still alive. As for Maurice's family, there must still be descendants somewhere. *If I could just talk to them, make them understand, then they could connect with Edith. They could right the wrong. Better late than never.*

Even though she hadn't worked out the exact details of how to execute it, Michele turned the plan over in her head. Yes, it really was the only way. She tried to guess how Edith's life had turned out; she would be in her sixties now. Perhaps she had become a nurse or a teacher. Those would have been popular careers for women of her generation. Maybe she had gotten married and had children of her own. Even if she didn't really want or need any money now, she should know what happened and have the opportunity to ask questions. Michele had to be the one to make the connection; no one else would.

First, though, she had to get back to the archives and learn more. She opened the front door and went inside. Janice was perched on the chair behind the Reference Room desk, clacking away on the keyboard. Michele pursed her lips. It was going to feel like forever until she could get back at it, or until the end of her shift—whichever came first. Hiding her annoyance, she approached the desk. "Good morning. Looks like you're already into things."

She watched her boss's lips undulate as presumably they read the last sentence on the screen. Seemingly satisfied, Janice paused her typing and turned her attention to Michele. "Hey, how are you today?"

"I'm a little tired. Busy evening yesterday." *Yes, busy reading an old diary that has taken over my life for some inexplicable reason. No big deal.*

"Oh yeah? Anything exciting?" Janice asked.

Michele paused for a second before responding. She would fill Janice in, but not yet. There was still more to find. "No, nothing really. Just the usual. Life with a five-year-old." She shrugged.

"Of course. I remember those days," said Janice. "It's a special time."

"Right." Michele changed direction. "But I'm ready to get back at that inventory."

"Excellent. I'll leave you to it." Janice returned to the keyboard. Michele placed her backpack behind the desk and went into the vault. She had to continue researching the diary, but obviously it wasn't going to be now. For the time being, she did the only thing she could: she found her list and pencil from the day before and started checking boxes. The hours crawled along.

From time to time Michele opened the door a crack to check if Janice might be leaving; it pained her to not look every five minutes, but she managed to stretch the intervals to half an hour. At long last, she saw a possible opportunity. Janice had stood up from the computer and picked up her purse; she was probably getting ready to go across the parking lot to buy her habitual lunch of Vietnamese spring rolls with vermicelli and grilled tofu. Michele opened the door wide and walked out as nonchalantly as she could manage, making a show of looking at the clock as she entered the Reference Room. "Oh, looks like we both had the same idea. I guess it's that time!"

Good grief, I sound ridiculous, she thought.

Janice smiled as she slung her purse strap over her shoulder. "I guess so! Do you want to go first? I could stay, I really don't mind."

"No! I mean, no, you go ahead. I haven't been too hungry during the day lately. But I wouldn't be opposed to a change in scenery for a bit. I'll watch the desk."

"OK, if you're sure." Janice pulled her sunglasses out of her purse and balanced them on her head before heading for the front door. "I'll be back soon."

Michele waved and called out after her, "Take your time!" After racing to the window to confirm that Janice had left, she scrambled to her backpack. She coaxed the copies out like a magician performing a trick. Instead of a string of silk scarves or a white rabbit, she drew out the diary pages and set them on the desk. She stretched her neck around the edge to make sure no one was coming in. The coast was clear, and she darted to the vault and disappeared inside. Remembering that she needed to keep an eye on the Reference Room, she picked up a brown rubber wedge from the floor. She propped open the door, hurried to the processing table, and picked up the diary. She knew the contents pretty well now, but whenever she held it, she still felt a familiar yet strange sensation. Once again she studied the cover, front and back, before revisiting each page. This sequence had become something of a sacred ceremony that she had to perform every time, whether it was with photocopies or the original.

Engrossed in Clotilde's words, Michele didn't hear the front door open. She had just closed the diary when Janice popped into her field of vision. *Why is she here?* She swiftly tucked the book into a box and faced Janice as she came towards her.

"The restaurant was closed, so I decided to skip lunch. I'll just leave early today instead. What have you got in there?"

"That? Oh, just that recent discovery I mentioned." Michele arranged some items on the table. "I thought there might be some time to do a bit of research on it today. Of course, it's not the priority—like you said before. But I wanted to have it on hand during your lunch in case I ran out of other work." She stumbled over her words. "It can totally wait. Obviously. I don't want to do anything that will hurt our case in this whole review process. Numbers and all that."

Janice eyed her for a moment. "It must be quite the find. I appreciate you being able to restrain yourself. I'm sure you'll be able to get to it soon enough. Have you found anything out yet?"

"You know, it's tricky with the translation, so I haven't gotten too far. But I'll let you know." *Once I have all the information, that is.*

"Sure, that's fine," Janice replied absently, already heading back to work at the reference desk. "Oh, and I have that key for you, if you're wanting to be here after hours. It's in the filing cabinet. Take it when you're ready.

No matter how good her intentions, Michele hated holding out on Janice, who had always been a good boss. But it made sense to get the full picture before filling her in. She closed the box. Once more she had no choice but to work on the inventory.

When Janice left for the day with a short good-bye, Michele returned to the Reference Room to start her research. With half an hour until closing time, she tried to determine where to begin. How could she research people without knowing any of their last names? The vertical files could be helpful, but she would have to use the finding aid to see if there were matches on any of the first names, and then go through each of those files to determine whether or not they represented any of the people on her list. That could mean a lot of folders; it was not the most efficient way to research. Trying to use the subject files would be even more like searching for a needle in a haystack. The World War Two file might have something related to Philippe's unit, or home front efforts at the Salvation Army, but it was more likely the information would be too broad. So often it took only one little detail to break a search wide open, but right now that key was missing. There just *had* to be a way to narrow down the possibilities.

She took a fresh piece of scrap paper from the stack and again wrote down what she knew. First names. A few wartime details. The fact that the families were French-speaking from France. She drummed the edge of the desk with the pencil. *What else?* Her forehead creased as she pushed her mind to recall more. *Wait!* St. Andrew's. Clotilde had attended the Roman Catholic Cathedral downtown. Maybe they had records that would identify her. It was a lead to follow, but it didn't help in the moment. Michele would have to contact their archives and make an appointment to visit. Unfortunately if they were anything like most small, private archives, they were probably accessible to researchers only during her work hours. She made a face. She could not afford to take time off right now. Maybe she could send them an email. After all, she responded to online inquiries all the time; they might be willing to do the same. She made a note to look for a website for St. Andrew's or the Roman Catholic Diocesan office and see about finding an email address to try. In the meantime, she thought as she fidgeted, she would have to focus on other sources.

She checked the time: ten minutes past the end of her shift already. She got up and closed the front door, but then sat back at the desk. Maybe she could stay a bit longer, since Janice had already approved it. Mrs. Eliades would be OK for a little while. Michele bumped the computer mouse to wake up the screen and lined her fingers up on the keyboard. *OK, let's see if we can find anything in the vertical files.* Determined, she opened the finding aid, went to the search function, and entered the first name: Clotilde. No results found. It had been a long shot to get a hit right away. Michele continued down her list. There were seventeen matches for Maurice, and many more files that had only the *M* initial. "This finding aid needs some work," she remarked. She moved onto Philippe. Again, no results, but when she shortened it to Philip, there were thirty-two. *Drat.* That was almost as bad as none. *Alright, how about this?* She typed "Edith" and then hit her head on the desk in exasperation when she saw the number fifty-three. She needed more time.

She uncurled herself from the desktop, picked up the phone, and dialled. While it rang, she braced herself for the response she would receive from the other end of the line. She never phoned home, and Mrs. Eliades' first instinct was always to assume that a call meant bad news.

"Hello! Speak, please!" Mrs. Eliades' voice thundered through the receiver.

"Hi, it's Michele. I—" she began.

Mrs. Eliades cut her off with a flurry of questions. "Michele? What's wrong? You OK? You come home soon? What happened? Oh my God, something happened!"

Michele tried to put her at ease, but it was hard to get a word in. Finally, she managed to say "No, no, I'm fine. I promise."

"You fine? Then why you calling?" Mrs. Eliades responded. Her tone had become suspicious.

"Well, um, I need to work late tonight." Michele cradled the receiver between her cheek and shoulder and scrolled through the finding aid on the computer screen. There were so many names to investigate. She needed to think beyond today. "Actually, probably every night for the rest of the week. Maybe even the weekend too. My boss has asked me to put in extra hours to work on a … really important project." She cringed at the lie.

Mrs. Eliades gasped. "Michele, that's too much, no? And what about the boy?"

"Actually, that's why I'm calling. I'm hoping Henry can hang out with you. I mean, I know he already does, but … more. It's just for a few days."

An awkward silence hung in the air between them. It felt like a long time before Mrs. Eliades spoke. "He misses you, you know that, Michele? He is a sweet boy. He needs his mother." Michele squirmed in the office chair and said nothing. After an uncomfortable moment, Mrs. Eliades gave her answer. "Fine. We will spend more time together. He is a good helper. But," she paused, "just for this week." Before Michele could thank her, Mrs. Eliades added, "I do this because I like him, yes, but also because I want you to make the extra money. I hope you no forget about our little talk the other day. On the first day of September you pay me all the rent, that's it."

Michele gulped. "Yes, thank you." Then she hung up. Now the lie was worse because she wasn't actually getting paid. Her boss hadn't even assigned this special "project." But what was done was done. She would have to solve the rent issue later. For now, she had to start pulling files. It was going to be another late night.

* * *

Thursday, August 13, 2009

Michele had spent hours on Wednesday afternoon and evening writing down the names of every Maurice and Philip that had a file, and starting the slow process of reading through them one by one. A surprisingly high number had had last names that looked obviously French or could possibly be French, but at least it had whittled them down.

When she arrived at home, eyes dry and irritated after too much focusing, Henry was already in his Spider-Man pyjamas. He rushed to her and squeezed her mid-section as tightly as he could before running upstairs and calling to her to follow. Distracted from all the information floating inside her head, she was considering just flopping herself onto the couch when Mrs. Eliades popped her head out of the kitchen with a hard stare and withdrew again without a word. A pang of guilt hit Michele, followed by that familiar feeling of being completely lost. What could she possibly know about parenting?

"Mummy, come *on*!" Henry yelled from the top of the staircase. Step by step, she went up to meet him and then read him a story from the Thomas the Train series. Then a thought struck her. Maybe being a mother could be approached the same way as that bedtime— one step at a time.

But when she returned to the archives on Thursday morning, she thought only of getting through the day so she could continue her research. She went through the motions, reconciling the inventory list with the boxes on the shelves. The diary remained out of sight on the processing table. Janice made a couple of attempts at friendly conversation, but Michele, worried about saying something stupid, engaged as little as possible. She hoped Janice wouldn't notice the new distance between them. *Or that I've completely gone off the rails the past few days.*

The change was dramatic, at least to Michele. When she came back from a trip to the restroom and saw there was only half an hour to go before closing time, she could feel herself start to transform like a werewolf at the first rays of moonlight. She always became obsessed with all the archival inquiries that came in, but even she could see this was excessive. It was more than she'd ever experienced, and it was taking over. She didn't understand it. All she knew was that she couldn't stop. She had to see this one through to the end.

"Michele? Can I talk to you for a minute?" Janice had shown up at her side, making her jump.

Michele brought her hand to her chest to slow her pounding heart. "Gosh, I'm sorry, Janice. I didn't see you there."

Janice frowned, visibly concerned. "Are you OK? I haven't wanted to pry, but you've seemed a bit off this week, like something's weighing on you. I know I'm your boss, but I also think of us as friends. If there's anything I can do, just let me know."

"Thank you, really. I appreciate that a lot. It's ... family stuff." Well, *someone's* family. She managed a smile. "I promise I won't let it affect my work."

"I'm not worried about that. You're great! But," Janice hesitated, "speaking of work, I do have an update for you. Let's have a seat." Her expression was kind as they took their places at a reference table. Michele waited for her to speak. Whatever it was, she could handle it. The only thing that mattered now was solving the mystery of the diary. Everything else was secondary.

"So," Janice continued. "I've heard back on my appeals about your position, and unfortunately they were only partially successful. Upper management is still going to reduce your hours in September, but only for a couple of months and then they will reassess the impact to the archives. Knowing that the fall is our busiest time—which I tried to tell them—I'm sure they will bump you back up after the trial period. I'm really sorry." When Michele didn't answer, Janice added, "I would be happy to give you a good reference if you want to look for other work. I don't want to lose you, but I would understand if you found better hours elsewhere. Or if you can get some more part-time work, we can arrange things so you can do both jobs. And you're still welcome to come in and do that research, even if you go. I'll help in any way I can."

Michele's voice came out strong and calm, and it surprised her to hear it that way. It was as if she were having an out-of-body experience. "Thank you for trying. It means a lot. I knew this could be the outcome, and it's fine. I mean, it's not *fine*—obviously I want to work more here, not less—but I'll figure something out." In response to Janice's doubtful expression, she added, "Really, I'm OK." She looked at the clock. "Don't you have to get going?"

"I do, actually. I have an appointment to get to. But I can lock up, if you need some time after that bad news."

"You go ahead. I'm going to take you up on that offer to stay after hours," Michele insisted.

"Alright. See you tomorrow, and hang in there."

When Janice had left, Michele went straight to the vertical files and slid the folded list of names from the back pocket of her black pants. Two days ago, when Janice told her about the proposed cutbacks, Michele had been devastated. Now it seemed like so long ago, and she didn't have time to be upset. In fact, more than ever she needed to make the most of her time at the archives. She pushed her financial and career worries far to the back of her mind to await a future plan. She opened and closed drawers in the first filing cabinet and pulled out a few files, carrying on from where she had left off the day before. Instead of putting them on the table, she took them to the desk and sat down facing the computer. She had not forgotten about reaching out to St. Andrew's. The vertical files would keep her going for a while and the cathedral might not have anything for her, but she had to try. No stone left unturned.

After finding their website and writing down the general email address, she logged onto her personal email and hit the Compose button. She explained as clearly as she could, without sounding desperate, that she was doing some genealogical research and was searching for the last name of a parishioner from the 1940s named Clotilde. Could they possibly check their membership rolls as soon as possible? It was a time-sensitive matter and she would be most grateful for their assistance. She read her message back. *Perfect. If I were the one receiving this inquiry, I would be intrigued.* Send. *Now please let them come back with something. I need this.* It could take only one detail to set her on the right track, and she couldn't shake the feeling that the clue she needed just might be there waiting within the church's red brick walls.

* * *

Friday, August 14, 2009

Thursday evening's efforts hadn't brought any results. Michele had not found any matches, and she hadn't received a response from St. Andrew's yet. Of course, she knew their office had already been closed for the day when she emailed them, but it hadn't stopped her from refreshing her inbox every few minutes. Even though a breakthrough had not come, however, she had felt a renewed hope for her search when she got up on Friday.

The archives had been unexpectedly busy all morning, with researchers in and out since first thing, but it had been a pleasant diversion. It had only just slowed down in the last fifteen minutes.

Now that the Reference Room was quiet and she'd returned to the vault, she hummed "I Gotta Feeling" by the Black Eyed Peas, the hit song all over the radio of late. Maybe tonight would be a good night for her. Maybe tonight would be the night she found Clotilde. Michele had already plotted out which files she would try after work, committing the day's names to memory. She felt her spirits rise with the music and threw herself into the inventory assignment as she waited out the last hour. After spending time overnight reflecting on the past few days, she had convinced herself there was no reason to be so nervous. Mind over matter. She just had to focus on regular archives duties during work hours, knowing she could go hard on her personal project *after* hours. Now it was nearly that time. She had to be patient for only a little while longer. Nothing could bring her down.

When Janice came into the vault to retrieve a box, Michele didn't flinch at all. *Yes! I've so got this. Eyes on the prize.* Before Janice took the box out to the Reference Room, she stopped and said, "Hey, you seem more chipper today. I hope that means your family situation is resolved?"

"I think it's going to be OK, thank you." Michele felt her shoulders relax. "I'm feeling much better today."

"I'm so glad to hear that. And you know what? I think you should take off early. I insist." Janice beamed.

Michele hadn't anticipated a curveball. "Wait, what?"

"Yes, go home! It's Friday, and you've been staying late all week. I've left early a couple of times, so it's only fair."

"Uh, I don't know."

Janice wouldn't take no for an answer. "Well, I do know. Take a break from the research. Clean up back here, come and grab your paycheque, and then head out. Go enjoy the weekend with your family." She seemed pleased with herself as she left.

"Um, OK. Um. Thank you. I'll just … put my stuff away. And grab that key. For next time." The relief of getting paid was tempered by the order Janice had just delivered. *OK, what am I going to do now?* She closed her eyes and took three deep, long breaths to refocus. *I really need another session with the files. And if I'm going to be doing research this weekend at the library, I have to be able to cross-reference the information I find.* She slowed down and tried to separate out the wheat from the chaff of her thoughts.

Michele knew what she had to do. Besides, Janice had already offered her the key and given her permission to dig into the diary on her own. Michele didn't need to be with her family or take a break from her research. She needed answers. What Janice didn't know wouldn't hurt her. Michele entered Janice's office, opened the third drawer of the filing cabinet, and reached to the very back until her fingers made contact with the uneven metal of a set of keys. With that, she strode out into the Reference Room. Michele scooped up her cheque from the desk before threading her arm through the backpack strap and lifting the bag over her shoulder. "Thanks again," she said, and walked out the door.

* * *

Sunday, August 16, 2009

On the weekend, Michele stuck to her plan. For two days she travelled between the archives and the main library branch, where she jumped between the History Room and her favourite computer station hidden in the farthest possible corner. She didn't want any prying patrons wondering about the old-looking writing on the pages beside her. Her eyes crossed with data from genealogical websites, the sites of other local archives, and those of more far-reaching organizations like Library and Archives Canada. She searched through military records documenting World War Two deaths, but once again couldn't get very far without a last name. Michele lost all perception of time as she dove down one rabbit hole after another like Alice in Wonderland. She had been home only to sleep and hadn't seen Henry or Mrs. Eliades for more than a few minutes at a time. At this stage, it was probably for the best. But on Sunday when the closing announcement came on thirty minutes before the library would shut its doors for the night, she deflated. She had nothing.

All her research tricks had gotten her nowhere. The only lead she had left was St. Andrew's. She'd been so caught up in the library resources that she had forgotten to check her email. With the clock in the bottom right corner of her screen pushing her on, she logged onto her account and watched as new messages populated her inbox. She skimmed past a note from Amanda, an archives mailing list conversation about storage solutions, and a lot of spam. There, in the middle of them all, was the only email she wanted to see. She clicked it open and read.

Dear Michele, thank you for your inquiry. We did have a look in our records for you and found a reference to only one Clotilde in our member rolls for the 1940s. We could not locate any other information on her, but we can tell you that her last name was Joseph. We hope that you find this information useful, and best of luck with your search. Sincerely, Mary.

Joseph! Clotilde finally had her name back. Michele felt faint with effort. This was the information that would change everything, she just knew it. But she had to be sure. She crammed her notebook and pencil in her backpack, gently added the copied diary pages, and then checked the front pocket for the keys. Speed-walking out of the library so as not to be reprimanded by staff, she tripped out the doors and then ran like her life depended on it. She raced for the bus but later wouldn't remember getting on it. The story surrounded her— it was all she could see until she reached the archives and found herself standing at the entrance with the key in the lock.

This is it. She had to know, and now she had a solid lead. Hands at her sides, she approached the filing cabinets like an adventurer about to uncover their greatest discovery. She went to the J drawer and pulled it out ever so slowly, as if even the slightest wrong move could set off unknown traps.

She held her breath. She flew past the names, registering only a couple of them along the way—James, Johnson—until she reached Joseph. There would not be a Clotilde; Michele had already checked the finding aid. But maybe, just maybe, there was someone just as important. Her chest tightened, and then she found him: Joseph, Philip. Not Philippe, but spellings could be fluid in records. It had to be him. She pulled out the file, suddenly afraid. *Don't be silly.* She shook her head. *I've come this far.*

Inside were copied documents about Philip's service in the Second World War: how his plane had crashed over Normandy; information about his grave, which was under the perpetual care of the Commonwealth War Graves Commission. The spelling on the latter confirmed it—it really was Philippe. She flipped through the pages until she reached the last, tiny piece of paper. It was an obituary from the *Colonist* with "November 1980" scrawled across the top.

JOSEPH, Clotilde. Died in Victoria on November 11 after a short illness. Born in Poitiers, France, on September 19, 1922 and a resident of Victoria for 45 years. Clotilde was a devoted member of St. Andrew's Cathedral and will be missed by the members of the Catholic Women's League. Predeceased by her husband Philippe, who was killed in the Second World War. She is survived by her only daughter, Edith Norman (Dan) and beloved baby granddaughter, Michele.

A jagged shriek caught in Michele's throat, cutting her open to her raw core. She had always been Michele Norman and nothing beyond that. Independent. No attachments. But now that same Michele Norman was a daughter and a granddaughter. Suddenly this was not just an archives story. It wasn't someone else's story. It was hers.

CHAPTER 5

September 8, 1946

You read me like music. You know my every glance like no one else—I do not need to say a single word. I was frightened to open myself to you, to expose my every sad note. But you encourage me to share all of them. When I criticize my highs and lows, you tell me that they are beautiful. You hear the song as a whole and explain that all of the parts are essential. They are all part of me.

I wish that I had your keen ear. Like a conductor, you patiently guide me. I am learning to listen. Every evening in front of the small fire, Edith balances herself, mesmerized, on the arm of the sofa as you play your violin. You never hold back, and this concept is so strange to me. When you pass the bow over the strings, you are pure emotion; you and your instrument are one. Tonight the room grows too warm, but I do not move from beside the hearth. The season is second to the flame. I watch your face and your eyes close as the melody swells. My cheeks burn.

* * *

Monday, August 17, 2009

For hours, Michele was numb. Somehow she had made it back to her quiet house and then had wandered from room to room to try to find a spot that felt right. Like a porcelain doll being arranged for display, she tried a variety of positions: prim and proper in the armchair, reclined on an oak step, flat on her back on top of her cold bed. Always her arms remained rigid at her side and she took care not to crack her fragile face. After midnight she gave up. She wouldn't be able to sleep that night—maybe not ever again. With a robotic arm she retrieved a light jacket from the hook by the front door and then jerked her way outside into the dark neighbourhood. Her energy level, already low, plunged to empty, and she found herself in the middle of a deserted Cloverdale Avenue staring at the shadowy streets and scapes she thought she'd known so well. Everything had changed. As she started back to the sidewalk, a black GMC pickup sped by, the driver leaning heavy on the horn.

It shook her out of her paralysis. "Whoa!" She jumped over the curb and glared at the truck travelling up the hill and into the night. *What am I doing? I have got to pull it together.* She drifted towards Rutledge Park. For the first time, she allowed herself to acknowledge the meaning of the words in Clotilde's obituary. *She is my grandmother. Edith is my—mother. My mother.* But why were her parents named in a local obit if they were transients like John and Barbara had said? Something felt off. She turned the details of her research over in her mind as she made her way towards the playground. Nothing she had discovered in the documents hinted that she'd been researching her own family all along—not until she found the newspaper clipping. The shadows cast by the streetlights emphasized the deep creases in her forehead. She threw herself up onto the pink elephant's back. None of this added up.

Michele let her legs slide back and forth along Rutley's smooth sides as she tried to approach the situation logically. She remembered how the diary had felt so familiar, how it had seemed to call out for her attention. How could that be? Could she have seen it as an infant or toddler, before she lived with Amanda? Henry still remembered details from when he was really young, so maybe it was possible? Had Edith—her mother—shown it to her? Had it only been a coincidence that Michele had been able to relate so strongly to

Clotilde's situation, that she'd felt so close to her? Had Michele's actions been the result of an archival obsession, or had she somehow known deep down that there was something more to it? And then there was the biggest question of all: what had happened to her family? There had to be more to the story than what she'd been told. The obituary said "beloved baby granddaughter." She hugged herself. She didn't know why her parents had abandoned her, but now she knew someone had loved her. The realization was stronger than any resolve to be analytical. Tears came, coating her face like a balm.

When they petered out, she jumped down onto the grass and considered her next steps. Although her understanding had changed, her mission to make things right had not. The difference now was that it was personal. She had to know the truth, no matter what the cost. Maybe not receiving the money from Maurice's family after his death had had such a significant impact on her grandmother and mother that it had ultimately determined the events leading to her own confused childhood. *Or even to this moment right now, in this park,* she thought. Alone in the early morning hours while her child was home in bed. It was possible. She had to find the answers, whatever they might be. For the first time, she would not turn away.

Before she could contact Maurice's family, she had to find one more last name. She couldn't wait until the library opened in order to do the research. Time was in short supply; technically her workday would begin in a few hours, although she couldn't bring herself to think about that just yet. What she needed was access to a computer, and fast. But what would be open at midnight, and nearby? She returned to Cloverdale and set her sights on the bright Blanshard Street intersection. At the corner she spotted the answer—the Accent Inn, lit up like a beacon of hope. Michele rushed towards it, the building's blue trim coming into view as she passed the neighbouring cable company's brick call centre. Motels were open twenty-four hours, right? This one had to have a computer in the lobby. And a phone. There were too many questions, and she couldn't move forward without answers. It was important enough to justify a middle-of-the-night call. She checked all her pockets as she stood in the parking lot, the glow of the entrance guiding her search. Her fingers located a bill and she pulled out a crumpled five dollars. *Yes, that might do the trick.*

She yanked the door open and made straight for the front desk. The lobby was empty except for the night auditor leaning back in his office chair reading a day-old edition of the *Times Colonist*. She started to lose her nerve and contemplated making her exit when he folded a corner of the paper inward and addressed her.

"Can I help you with something?" His thin, pale face exuded a surprising friendliness.

"Hi … Hello. I'm really sorry to bother you, and this might seem like a strange request, but I'm wondering if I could use your phone for a local call? And your computer station?" She turned to indicate the small desk in the corner. "The deadline for my … paper … is tomorrow, and I realized that I missed something, and I don't have a computer at home." She could hear herself rambling but couldn't stop. "I live just up the street—I'm a neighbour, really—and I was hoping I could do this last bit of research here. I just need to check in with my partner first. I promise I won't download or upload anything. And here," she tried to flatten the sad bill on the counter. "I could pay for the time." Finally, she paused long enough to make eye contact.

Geoff, as his tag read, put the paper down and rubbed his eyes before speaking. "You know what? Sure, why not. I won't take the money as long as you promise not to tell anyone about this.

Wouldn't want people showing up off the street every night to use our equipment. It's supposed to be for guests only. Just keep a low profile."

"Thank you! I really can't thank you enough," she replied. Geoff had already returned to his newspaper. She gave him a wave even though he couldn't see it, rushed to the computer station, and lifted the phone's handset.

After four rings, John's groggy voice came through.

"Hello? Who is this?"

"Hi, it's Michele. I'm sorry to wake you."

"Michele? Well, hello there, stranger!" John's surprise cut her to the quick. Other than the obligatory calls at Christmas and Easter, she had not phoned or visited in ages. "You know you can call us any time, so don't worry about that. But it's real late. Is something wrong?" She heard movement. "Hold on a minute while I sit down. I'm tangled up in the cord of this old phone."

She pictured him settling by the front window in his rust-coloured armchair. During the day, the view from the condo could not compare to the rose garden Barbara had cultivated outside their house for decades, yet his decreasing mobility and her dementia diagnosis had precipitated the decision to move. But this call wasn't about roses.

There was no easy way to say it. "I know who my parents are. And maternal grandparents."

Silence. "But, how? We didn't … You didn't let us …"

"I found my grandmother's diary, but it was her obituary that confirmed things. But never mind that." Her tone hardened. "My parents weren't transients, were they. Did they actually abandon me? Wait, did you kidnap me? I need the truth."

"No, honey, it wasn't like that."

"Then tell me, what *was* it like. Has my whole life been a lie?"

Dead air met her, and she wondered if the connection had dropped. "Are you still there? Hello?"

"Yeah, I'm here," her adoptive father responded at last, choking up. "You just caught me off guard, that's all. I always told Barb that one day you'd come 'round asking questions. Didn't expect it to be today, but whatever brought you here, I'm glad for it. Of course, we'd practiced what we were going to say, but now that the moment's come I'm not sure where to start."

"Just tell me if they really left me at the church or not." Michele dropped her voice to a whisper when Geoff glanced up. "How about that?"

"Whatever you want, honey." John took a deep breath and began." First of all, you're right: they weren't transients. But they were in a bad way when they gave you up. Real bad. That part was true. They were ashamed about their circumstances. Embarrassed. And we did meet them through Sacred Heart. Both of them came for meals once in a while, and your mom attended services. She and Barb hit it off and they became like family. The women were overjoyed to be pregnant at the same time and helped each other through it, but money became more of an issue for your parents. Your dad kept his distance. I think he was overwhelmed. We offered to buy baby essentials for them, but they turned us down. And then you girls came along, and your mothers were convinced you two would be the best of friends just like they were. Things were tough for a lot of folks back then, but it was the happiest time of our lives in many ways."

Michele's lip quivered but she forced it still. "So, what happened?"

"The stress of trying to get enough work, providing for Edith and you—your dad couldn't handle it. He kept saying he was a failure. That it would be better if he were gone. By the time you were two, he had one foot out the door. He would disappear for longer and longer stretches." John cleared his throat and continued. "Your mom adored Dan. There was never going to be anyone else. There was no way your mom could look after you on her own. We knew there were money issues in the past as well. Didn't have all the details. So, before your dad left town for the last time, they asked us to adopt you. The only condition was that we tell you the altered version. They didn't want you to know."

Poverty and single mothers: the family legacy that kept on taking. Maybe it *would* have been better not to know. If it hadn't been for the diary, Michele wouldn't have gone down this road. But now that she *did* have the real story, her idea of making things right was more important than ever. It was a matter of figuring out how.

She ran her fingers through her hair. "Thank you. That's what I needed to know."

"There's more, if you want ..."

"No," she cut him off. "I've heard enough for today. I can't right now ... I'm sorry. You go back to bed, OK?"

"I know it's a lot to take in. You call me back when you're ready. I can talk, or just listen. Any time. You hear me?"

"I'll keep that in mind. Bye."

Jaw clenched, she sat at the computer. It was about more than making things right. It was about justice. And for that, she had to find Maurice. Janice had once observed that she had a kind of sixth sense when it came to research; Michele just hoped it wouldn't let her down this time when she needed it most. She fired up the machine and entered the URL for the online burial record database. This was no time for idle browsing—she had to dive right in. She typed the name, death date, and cemetery, and hit enter. Clotilde's burial record came up immediately. Michele wrote down the grave location using the hotel notepad and pen on the desk. Next, she looked for records from Royal Oak Burial Park with the first name Maurice. One by one, she compared the grave locations of each result with that of Clotilde's until she found what she'd been looking for: a Maurice with a) the same death year as the one noted in the diary, b) a French last name, and most importantly, c) a grave located right beside Clotilde's. She knew without a doubt that Maurice Bouchard was the man her grandmother had wanted to spend the rest of her life with.

Despite the fact it was so late, the discovery energized Michele. She opened a new tab and entered different search terms to learn more about Maurice and the Bouchard family business in France. For a moment a disconcerting thought popped into her head: what if it was no longer in operation? After weighing the possibility, however, she brushed it aside. Open or not, she would find them. She had come too far to give up now. She tried every word combination she thought might lead her to the answer: Maurice—Bouchard—business—France—1940s. On a whim, she added "Paris" and "financial" to the mix; she had no idea what kind of business she was looking for, but if the family had been as successful and well-off as she had gathered from the diary, then they may have been associated with investments, banking, or other financial ventures. At the very least, she might find a report or statement that would lead back to them.

She pressed enter again and waited. A list of links sprang up on the screen in front of her, and as Michele scanned them, the pattern was clear. They all pointed to the same place: *Compagnie Financière Bouchard*—Bouchard Financial Company—in Paris. She tried to contain her excitement. "OK, let's not get too excited yet. We don't have any proof this is the same family," she whispered. Realizing she had spoken aloud, she surveyed the room to see if anyone had heard her. Geoff was busy counting money behind the front desk and not a single soul had entered the lobby.

Satisfied that no one had taken notice of her, she clicked on the Bouchard website link. The home page was sleek. At the bottom, a banner boasted in French, "Providing financial services to France for over seventy years." A group of sharply dressed professionals stood with serious expressions and arms crossed. She supposed a prospective client would prefer a company that projected experience and importance. A stern man who she guessed was in his late eighties dominated the photograph. *He must be in charge. Let's see what we can learn about him.*

According to the About page she translated, the company was founded in the 1930s by two brothers, Maurice—her heart jumped—and Gérard Bouchard. "Starting from scratch at a young age, they used their resourcefulness, good sense, and determination to quickly grow a successful enterprise during challenging times." *Impressive.* She continued to read: "Sadly, Maurice died suddenly in 1949 in Canada. Gérard continued to build on their legacy and today remains at the helm of the Bouchard Financial Company, aided by his daughter, Berdine. We are proud of the achievements of this family business. We are once again in challenging times, but despite this, we have not only come through the latest economic crisis, but have also taken advantage of the opportunities it presented. Our business model continued to generate profits for our customers and shareholders. This achievement, along with our charitable work in support of families in need, recently earned us a nomination for the 2009 "Bank of the Year Awards" from *The Banker*. The recipient will be announced in November. We look forward to continuing to serve you."

Wow, definitely not a small business—I figured it was construction or something. And definitely prosperous. Michele reread the last two sentences. *Helping families? What a joke.* The thought renewed her anger over the greediness that had left her grandmother—and by extension, her mother—in hardship. *I need to know more about who I'm dealing with here,* Michele decided. She opened yet another tab and searched for any relevant news articles from the past ten years. There were more matches than she could ever read; from the first few, however, it was clear the Bouchard's were a prominent, wealthy family, long established in Parisian social and financial circles. Based on the accounts of some of their corporate takeovers, they were ruthless too.

She sat back and debated how to contact them. Emails were easily ignored, and phone calls could be redirected or blocked. *Think, Michele, think. They may be rich and influential, but your family is important too. They mattered. They still matter.* A radical idea sprouted in the back of her brain. The Bouchard's would never come to her; she would be lucky if they even acknowledged her existence. As she nurtured her idea, it formed branches and leaves and grew taller—just like the trees lining the boulevards in Paris. *Yes, Paris.* The only way to resolve this once and for all was to confront the Bouchard's in person. It would be harder to dismiss her if she were looking them in the eye. *This is crazy.* Yet as she admitted it, she made the decision to go. Greenery now filled her head, the notion firmly planted. She would speak with them face to face. Now she just had to find a way to get there.

With a start she remembered there was someone she knew who could probably help—Amanda. Michele had never asked her for anything. She'd never taken her up on any of her many offers—but this was important. And Scott, Amanda's adoring husband, worked for Air Canada. If anyone could get her a last-minute flight, it would be him. She checked the time on the lobby clock; it was 3:00 a.m. She closed all the tabs on the screen and cleared her browsing history before making one last visit to the front desk.

"I'm all finished now," she informed Geoff. "Thanks again for letting me use the phone and computer. You have no idea how much it meant to me."

The clerk seemed perplexed by the extent of her gratefulness. "Sure, no big deal. That conversation seemed pretty intense, so I hope you sorted things with your partner. Good luck with your paper."

"Right. My paper. Thanks, and good night!" There was so much to do and without a list to consult she felt scrambled. She darted along Cloverdale Avenue and back to Alder Street, slowing down as she moved up the front steps and into the house.

She crept up to the bedroom and pulled a small battered suitcase from the closet. Henry slept curled up on a nest of blankets and sheets, while Ares, tight against him, opened a vigilant eye. Michele gave the dog a pet to appease him and he returned to his slumber. She lay the suitcase out on her bed, went to her dresser, and pulled out clothes drawer by drawer. As she folded and fit everything into the luggage like pieces in a game of Tetris, she watched her son. She'd never been far away from him before. A peculiar feeling filled her chest. This trip was about her family—Henry's family, too. But it was also her opportunity to be like those girls from school, to finally have an adventure. It was what she had wanted for so long, but now that it was really happening, it didn't feel quite as she had expected.

Once she had finished packing, she didn't know what to do next. She wanted to keep moving but had to put her plan on hold until the morning; everyone she needed to speak with was still asleep. She wasn't going to wake anyone else tonight. Perhaps sleep would be the best thing to do, she thought as she let out a huge yawn. After setting the alarm for seven o'clock, she undressed and got under the covers. Even as her eyelids grew heavy, she still doubted whether she would be able to fall asleep. A kaleidoscope of images merged in front of her: a brown book, a woman and her daughter, the Eiffel Tower, a boy in a cape, her childhood home, a stuffed bunny, a pink elephant, a blue apron. She walked through a tunnel and emerged onto an airplane, but when she turned around, she was alone in a field. "I can't do this; it's too hard," she cried. A warning siren sounded in the distance and she sprang up to find her alarm going off. Three hours had passed in what seemed like three seconds. She wasn't sure if she felt better or worse for it.

The suitcase sat by the bedroom door, waiting. Michele put on a fresh outfit before grabbing the bag and carrying it downstairs. After leaving the luggage under the coat hooks, she tiptoed to the kitchen and listened. Mrs. Eliades was either out gardening or doing early morning cleaning jobs, or she was still in her room. Michele took the opportunity to make her first call. She dialled a number from memory and after three rings a harried female voice answered, "Hello?"

"Amanda? It's Michele."

The voice warmed. "Michele! Is something wrong? Not that I don't love hearing from you, but I'm just surprised."

"I'm sorry for phoning so early. I hope I didn't wake you up? I thought maybe the kids would be up and going by now, so I took a chance—"

"Callum, stop hitting your brother!" Amanda shouted into the distance. "Sorry about that. Yeah, we're definitely up, so no worries there. What's going on?"

Michele's shoulders tensed. Why was this so difficult? "I have a favour to ask. A really big one."

"Really?" Amanda sounded surprised. "Of course! You know that I am here for you. Always."

"Um, thanks. But you haven't heard what I'm asking for yet," Michele responded. She kept scratching her jawline even though it wasn't itchy.

"Michele, seriously. If I can help in some way, please let me."

"OK, but don't say I didn't warn you." It was time for the ask. "I need to go to Paris, today. Do you think Scott could get me a ticket? I'll take any route." She wavered but then explained, "I wouldn't ask if it wasn't important."

Amanda hesitated. "Paris? What's going on? Spill."

"I'm not ready to talk about it yet."

"That's ominous. Fine. I said I would help, and I meant it." Amanda sighed. "This must be really important, so I'm sure we can make it happen. I'll let you know when he's booked it but be ready to go to the airport. But Michele," she added. "What about Henry? Is he going too? And do you know your return date?"

They were reasonable questions, but they caught her unawares regardless. "Um, no. Just me. For about a week. It would be great if the return could be flexible, though."

"OK, fine. I don't know what's going on, but I hope you know what you're doing. And please, *please* be careful. You're my sister and BFF so I get to care double." It was something Amanda had said many times over the years.

"Thank you. I'll be ready for the flight."

As Michele hung up, Mrs. Eliades came in through the back door. "Flight? What you mean, a flight? Airplane? For who?" Her frown punched down into her chin.

Better to get this over with as soon as possible, Michele thought. "Something has … happened." *Not a great start.* "There's a family emergency and I have to leave right away. It's quite far, so I'll be gone for a week."

Mrs. Eliades pursed her lips, registering the announcement. "Family? You never mention any family. Now you go just like that? How you pay for this?"

Michele tried to explain herself without giving more away than necessary. "You're right, I haven't mentioned family because it's been only me for so long. But they just connected, and they need me. Someone else is making the arrangements, so you don't have to worry about what it's costing me. I know I still need to get you the rent, and I will, but I have to do this."

"And what about the boy? He go with you?"

"I know it's a lot to ask, especially after the last few days, but could he please stay with you? I don't have anyone else here who's able to look after him." Michele could see Mrs. Eliades was at her limit, but she persisted. "Please, I'm desperate."

Mrs. Eliades sighed. "OK, I do it. Didi and Henry, we have fun this week. But things gonna have to change when you get back, Michele. It's too much, for everyone." She walked away without another word and returned to the yard.

Michele couldn't dwell on the conversation. She had to make another call. From the bits of paper tucked beside the phone she pulled out the one she needed and dialled again.

"Hello?"

"Hi Janice, it's Michele."

"Oh, hi! Is everything OK? Not feeling well?" She sounded genuinely concerned; Michele wished she wouldn't be.

"I'm not sick, but I do have to leave town today for a family emergency. I don't really want to get into the details, but I'll be gone for about a week. I know it's sudden …"

Janice was congenial but Michele detected a touch of annoyance. "Oh. A week? Wow. Of course you have to go if it's an emergency. The timing is unfortunate, though, because I'm trying to show the city that your position is essential. But if you have to go, you have to go."

"Thank you so much. I'm sorry if this makes things difficult for you. I really do appreciate you trying to save my job. I can see that it's not an ideal time for this. I don't know what else to say." Maybe some honesty would help smooth things over.

"No, it's fine. Family comes first. I completely understand that. Just let me know when you get back, and I hope it all works out."

"I will. Thanks again. Bye." It was done. The path to Paris had been cleared.

The phone rang almost immediately with its urgent, shrill call. When Michele answered, Amanda's voice came through from the other end, buffered by the sound of screaming children.

"Hey, so you're good to go. Your flight to Vancouver leaves in two hours. You'll need to make another connection after that before you're on your way to Paris, but that was the only way to make it happen today. All you have to do at the airport is give your name and show your passport; they'll have the booking there. And Scott and I really wanted to make sure you had what you needed so we went ahead and made a hotel reservation with our credit card. He got a great rate, so we don't mind paying. Have you got a pen? Write down this address."

Michele obeyed and recorded the name and location. She had not even stopped to consider where to stay. If Amanda hadn't taken care of it, Michele would probably have wasted a lot of precious time wandering around trying to find accommodation. Asking her for help had been a good—though difficult—idea.

Shoving the address in her pocket, she rushed through the living room and up the stairs. She needed to gather a few more things before she got on the bus for the ride to the airport. In the bedroom, Henry wore a pair of khaki cargo pants backwards, matched with a stained Batman T-shirt. His eyes became jubilant when his mother came in the room. "Mummy, I'm so good at getting dressed now. Look!"

An unexpected tenderness came over her. "You are! I'm so impressed." She circled her arms around him and squeezed until he squirmed.

"Mummy, that's a very big hug!"

"It is. A big hug for my special guy. But now Mummy needs to talk to you about something, OK?" She sat on the bed and patted the spot beside her. Henry obliged. "Henry, I need to go away for a few days to deal with something very important. Now, I don't want you to be scared while I'm gone. Didi is going to look after you, and I'll be back soon, I promise."

"I get to be with Didi? Yay! I love Didi. Can I go play with my cars now?" Henry glided off the bed and ran to his toy bin, leaving Michele alone.

I don't think he's even going to miss me. The awareness twisted her up inside in a way she had never felt before. Pushing through the discomfort like a runner mid-race, she retrieved her pristine passport and put it in the front pocket of her backpack; the diary pages still rested in the main section at the centre. She examined the room in case she had missed anything, and her eyes landed on Henry driving his cars across the crowded floor. The pain struck a sharp blow to her gut. She could not ignore it this time. She jumped over an obstacle course of clothes and action figures and pillows until she was beside him, pulling his little warm mass against hers, kissing his smooth forehead and memorizing the youthful sweetness of his wild hair. The indulgence lasted a minute before she cut it off. It was already more than she had permitted herself in as long as she could remember. Now it was time to go.

* * *

From Victoria, Michele hopped to Vancouver before flying to Toronto. She dozed in between meals of cookies and pretzels and ginger ale. The in-flight purchases and the food offerings at Pearson Airport during her layover were not worth the money; everything would have to be done on the cheap this week if she was going to make it through. At least during all the travel she could ruminate over her vague plan and try to firm it up somehow. Eventually, the Air Canada gate agent made the pre-boarding announcement for the Paris flight, triggering Michele to stand up and gather her bags. It was the last chance to change her mind. After she got on that plane, she would be on her way across the ocean and to another country. Over the speakers she heard her row being called to board. She reread the crinkled boarding pass in her hand and then peered out the floor to ceiling windows at the huge jet parked outside. She slung her backpack over her shoulder. She was ready for takeoff.

Let's see ... Nine, ten, eleven ... twelve. Here we go. She located her row and was disappointed to find she'd been assigned the centre seat. *Beggars can't be choosers*, she reminded herself. At least no one was on the aisle side yet. She eased her backpack under the seat in front of her—she didn't like the idea of the copied diary pages in the overhead compartment, out of easy reach—and then sat back. Her seatbelt fastened, she assessed the passenger beside her at the window.

He had not acknowledged her presence at all, despite the fact that the seats were so close together. It wasn't like he didn't know she was there. It seemed rather unfriendly. Wasn't the polite minimum to at least make eye contact when you were going to be spending hours confined together in a small space? As they made their ascent, she took note of his pleated pants and tucked-in golf shirt. He was dressed simply and neatly, but his shoes and watch looked expensive. While his light brown hair was short and well-groomed, it had a bit of a messy style. So far, her preliminary research of her neighbour was inconclusive. She was so focused on this new inquiry that she did not think to move over into the still-empty aisle seat.

The stranger pulled out a book and immersed himself in it. *Aha, a clue!* Michele leaned forward and squinted her eyes as she attempted to make out some of the text. *Seriously, it's in French?* She grimaced. Then again, she *was* on a flight to France, so of course there would be French speakers on board. Duh. She craned her neck to study the cover. The stark design did not appeal to her, and the title confirmed her suspicion that the book was no novel: *Manuel d'histoire du droit français.* Who read about the history of law for fun? He was probably working, she supposed, but nevertheless it was a poor travel choice in her opinion.

Without warning, he pivoted his head to her, his left eyebrow raised in a question. "*Excusez-moi? Je peux vous aider?* Excuse me? Can I help you?"

She felt a burning lapping up her cheeks like flames out of control. "Oh! Um, oh! I'm so sorry. I mean, *désolée.* I mean, *je suis désolée.*" She hid her face in her clammy hands. *Oh, gosh. Is it too late to jump out of this airplane?*

"*Ne vous en faites pas.* Don't worry about it." His kind, reassuring voice encouraged her to open her fingers. Jewelled green eyes laughed back at her, emphasizing faint crow's feet at their corners. She lowered her hands and rubbed them along her jeans. Even though she was still mortified, she dared to take in his face. He still displayed the earlier intense expression, but a dimple gave away a lighter side. Maybe she had misjudged him, but it was hard to tell. So far, he was a jumble of contradictions and she did not know quite what to make of him. She debated introducing herself. It would be the adult thing to do. But before she could, he had stuck his head back in his book. She took the hint. *I guess I won't have someone to talk to. That's fine. I'll just entertain myself.* She stared at the back of the seat in front of her.

The first half of the trans-Atlantic flight felt like an eternity. With no one to chat with, Michele watched other passengers, like the elderly couple in the next row across the aisle unpacking and sharing the turkey sandwiches and potato chips they had brought on board. Glasses of wine from the first round of in-flight service complemented their meal. When the drink cart reached row twelve on the second round, her quiet seatmate ordered a glass of white wine. She wasn't sure, but she thought it might have been the pricier one available. She didn't drink often, but some fortification sounded really good right about now, after everything that had happened and everything to come. Her body followed with envy as the flight attendant handed him the wine. Michele had resigned herself to ordering yet another ginger ale when her neighbour eyed her inquiringly. She nodded and he asked for a second glass of the brilliant, straw-yellow liquid. In only a split second he'd asked her if she would like to partake and had known the answer without any words exchanged. She found it unnerving.

He held up his glass and toasted "*Santé*" before clinking hers. Suddenly shy, she muttered "Cheers" and then took a swig before thanking him for the drink. He shrugged nonchalantly and savoured the first slow sip. "It is nothing. Enjoy it." His eyes danced even though his body language was indifferent.

I don't get this guy, she thought. And yet, there was something about him. Purple crescents hung under those seas of green. His face was tired but handsome, his body tense but somehow relaxed. She took in every detail, curious, and then realized he was also observing her. She felt exposed, as if he could read her inside and out in one glance. Fighting the instinct to turn away, she held out her hand instead. "I'm Michele, by the way."

He took her outstretched hand and held it for a moment before taking another sip of wine. "Ah, Michele. *Un joli nom.* My name is Sébastien. You are from Toronto?"

"No, I'm from Victoria, British Columbia. On the West Coast of Canada." She had no idea if people from outside the country were familiar with it.

Sébastien bobbed his head. "It is near Vancouver, *non*? I heard that it is very beautiful there. I would like to visit someday."

"You should!" She thought she sounded too eager, so she backed off. "It's a great place, but it's expensive to live there. Very lovely, though."

"Like Paris as well. It is a wonderful city. Very famous of course, many things to see. And very costly also."

"Wow, do you live there?" she asked, amazed.

He looked out the window at the passing clouds. "Yes, I was born there. I have lived there for my entire life."

Her first conversation with a real Parisian! "So, what brought you to Toronto?" she inquired. She wondered if she was being too nosy. "I mean, it's none of my business. You don't have to tell me or anything."

He waved his hand in what she thought was a very French gesture. "No, no. *Ce n'est pas un secret.* In Paris we take our *vacances* in August. I had not been in Toronto before, and there was a law conference that I hoped to attend there, so I made the trip."

"You went to a work conference for your vacation?" she blurted. "No offence, but that doesn't seem like much of a getaway."

Sébastien digested her comment and gave his characteristic shrug. "Maybe not. But I had no other plans. This way I see some of Canada, and am educated in new legal developments. I am an— *avocat*. In English, you say lawyer."

Well, that explains the book. He seems too nice to be a lawyer, though. While Michele added this to her list of question marks about him, Sébastien posed more questions of his own.

"And Michele, may I ask why you are travelling to Paris? For the sightseeing?"

She downed more wine and was startled to find her glass nearly empty. She would never see him again after they landed, but she still wasn't comfortable discussing the details of her mission. "It's a long story. Basically, I'm doing some family research."

"Ah, la *généalogie?*"

"Sort of. Not exactly. But I'm trying to sort some things out about my family history."

Sébastien raised his thick eyebrows. "It must be very important for you to come all the way to France, *non?*"

"Yes. You have no idea. This trip is the only way to accomplish what I need to do." She yawned.

He watched her try to stretch within the boundaries of her seat, his eyes taking on a softness she did not register through the fatigue taking hold. "*Eh bien*, well in that case I should leave you to rest. It sounds like you will need your energy for this project." Their eyes locked and her instinct told her Sébastien inexplicably saw right through her while she couldn't seem to understand him at all.

He slumped back and dove into the law text once again. *Fine.*
Dismiss me. The French really are rude. It's just as well that the flight
will be over soon. She settled herself low in her seat and did her best
to get comfortable. The white noise of the engine and the wine sitting
warm in her belly sent her eyelids fluttering down like delicate
butterflies. As they descended, her neck arched until her head found
a strong shoulder and she fell into a deep sleep.

CHAPTER 6

I do not know how I would have made it through the past year without the help of Maurice. When I had no one else, there he was, as steady and calm as the ocean in Cadboro Bay on a summer's evening. The women at St. Andrew's have been charitable, of course, but they look at me always with concern on their faces and their expressions are reminders of what I have lost. Maurice has supported me without pity in his eyes. He is simply there, a warm presence without judgement.

How does one get through this life without the help of family and friends? It has been said again and again through history, I am sure, but truly there is no greater gift than a friend in difficult times. Maurice has been that to me and I will never forget the kindness that he has shown, especially when my words and actions have been at the mercy of trauma and emotion. I do not deserve his patient attention, but it is my lifeline. I only hope that one day I will find a fitting way to express to him my profound gratitude.

* * *

Wednesday, August 19, 2009

It felt like she had been hit by a truck. Michele's head swelled like a balloon filled to the bursting point. She groaned and flopped an arm forward so that it dangled off the side of the bed. Every joint ached as she moved. Suddenly she bolted upright, pain shooting through her limbs, and checked the clock radio. *I forgot to set an alarm! I have to get ready for work! Wait ... Where am I?* She looked around the room and realized it wasn't hers. There was no Henry spilling Hot Wheels across the floor. No Ares monitoring her in silent criticism. Even the sounds were all wrong; instead of the early tennis players at Rutledge Park and the clanging house pipes, she heard traffic and something like running water outside. *Paris! I'm in Paris.*

She flew to the window and ripped the drapes open. Men in green coveralls and reflective vests swept the street, directing the water flowing from curb-side valves and removing dirt and garbage that had accumulated the day before. Opposite the hotel, a solid mass of stone walls, carved wooden doors, and wrought iron balconies adorned with flower boxes greeted her—a living postcard. She took a long breath, stunned. It all seemed like a wonderful dream.

She checked the clock again and counted on her fingers. By her calculations, it must be Wednesday. She barely remembered arriving at the Hotel Magellan the night before, (which would have been morning in Victoria). When they landed at Charles de Gaulle airport, she had bid a polite "*au revoir*" to Sébastien before retrieving her belongings and joining the queue to deplane. He had looked at her strangely, she thought, but she chalked it up to travel fatigue— either hers, or his, or both. No matter. She had quickly lost him in the airport crowd. Not yet knowing how to navigate the public transportation system, she had used her credit card to pay for a shuttle to the hotel. She had presented her tattered scrap of paper with the name and address to the clerk.

"Ah, Le Magellan. It is in the seventeenth arrondissement, *oui?*"

Unsure, she had tried the shrug her neighbour had executed so successfully during the flight. Seemingly appeased, the clerk had muttered, "*Eh bien, on y va.*" She'd had her doubts, but in the end had been deposited at the front door with her bags. After a short shower she had thrown herself onto the hard bed. Not even the inflexible mattress could have stopped her from getting a complete night's rest at last, (though her body now complained bitterly).

Without warning her belly decided to join in the protest with a loud growl. Michele could not recall the last time she'd eaten a proper meal. She unzipped her suitcase and pulled out what she hoped was a fashionable summer outfit for her first day in Paris: denim shorts, flowy yellow top, and sandals. It was amazing what people donated to the thrift store. She was quite happy to benefit from their castaways. Clothes in hand, she read the tent card on the desk; apparently there was a breakfast room, and *le petit déjeuner* was included for all guests. Once she was dressed and ready, she headed down the single flight of stairs to the main floor and followed the signs to the dining area. A colourful selection of fresh and dried fruits, dispensers filled with various cereals, bowls of ice holding assorted yogurt cups, and trays of golden-brown pastries were spread out buffet style. There wasn't a bagel in sight. She picked up a shiny white plate from the top of a tall stack and surveyed the offerings, debating as to what might be the closest substitute for her regular morning fare.

She wrinkled her nose. After selecting a pain-au-chocolat and throwing in a vanilla yogurt and a ripe fig, Michele searched the dining room for a free seat. Travellers—mainly couples—were sprinkled amongst the tables and she didn't see how she could fit in with them. As she deliberated, the attendant charged with replenishing the food approached her.

"*Madame*, perhaps you would care to sit in our courtyard?"

Michele was grateful for the save. "*Oui, merci.* Thank you. Would you please show me the way?" Outside, she found an empty table shaded by a red umbrella. The sun was already scorching. She set herself down in a wicker chair and tore flaky chunks from her pastry, popping them in her mouth. The buttery layers melted together until she reached the semi-sweet chocolate baton at the centre. She closed her eyes. *Wow. This is nothing like my everything bagel. It's so much better.* She took her time and enjoyed every bite. After all, she didn't have a set schedule here.

But that, she realized after she had returned to her room to lock the diary pages in the safe and get her backpack, was a problem. Until now, her days had been fairly structured, balanced between work and parenting—and lately, research. Without a list, without a detailed plan, she had no idea where to go next. She hadn't really thought things through, which, come to think of it, contravened her usual *mode d'être*. Should she go directly to Bouchard Financial? Or maybe get her bearings first and figure out how to get around the city? Either way, she needed a map. She had a feeling of *déjà vu* as she neared the front desk, but instead of Geoff at the Accent Inn, this time a young lady in a smart suit stood behind the counter. Michele read the name tag, cleared her throat, and asked in formal French, "Excuse me, may I have a map please?"

The woman, named Maxine, gave her a professional smile and pulled several colour brochures out from under the desk. "Of course. I can give to you an excellent map of Paris, and also a plan for the Métro. Would you like some information on attractions to visit as well?"

"I'm actually here to work on a—research project. But sure, I'll take some just in case." Michele accepted all the offered pamphlets. It wouldn't hurt to compile as many facts as possible; you never knew when they might come in handy.

Maxine added, "I will be here every day this week, if you have any questions. All you have to do is ask."

"*Merci,*" Michele thanked her. *She's helpful, and she seems really nice too.* It was reassuring to know that Maxine would be a familiar face over the next few days. Of course, the front desk agent was just doing her job—she had to be cordial to all the guests. Besides, Michele wasn't looking for a friend. But perhaps this staff person would be a useful resource.

Michele pushed open the front doors and a wall of fire hit her as she stepped down to the sidewalk. Micro beads of sweat formed across her exposed skin. It felt much hotter than the courtyard. She took everything in. Just like when she'd first seen it from her window, the view stopped her in her tracks. To locals it was probably just an ordinary road, but to her, there was literally a world of difference between Rue Jean-Baptiste Dumas and Alder Street back home. While many older houses and apartment buildings populated her small corner of Victoria, here (and probably on all Parisian streets, she guessed), "old" had a completely different meaning: buildings throbbed with the generations of history that had been created within and around them, stories—cooling, soothing—cascading from the windows into the gorge formed by the stone structures. She could feel the arms of ancient residents reaching out from the balconies, calling her back into the shadows and beseeching her to listen. The invitations were deafening, but she could not accept them now. She had to continue on her orientation and after that, there was some other history she had already committed to discovering.

Clutching her maps, Michele took a left and wandered down the street. *I have no idea where I'm going. No big deal. No need to panic.* Perhaps once she reached the intersection, she could better assess her direction. Up ahead a blue and white sign advertised a paint and electrical shop, and across from it on the opposite side of Rue Jean-Baptiste Dumas stood a combination café/bar/convenience store. Was it a French thing to blend functions? She made a mental note to watch for more examples. When she reached the corner, she was disappointed to find both establishments dark and locked up tight. A barely legible hand-written note was taped on the door of the paint shop: "*Fermeture annuelle.*" She remembered something Sébastien had told her on the plane. He had said that the French take their vacations in August, right? If that were the case, then it followed that businesses would have their annual closures now. While it would have been fun to do some browsing this week, it wasn't like she was going to be doing much purchasing anyway—not on her budget.

At Rue Laugier, she studied her options. She looked left at the T intersection, straining her eyes to try to make out distant details. The street ended at a reddish-brown building that might have been brick. To her right it carried on much farther and appeared to open up in the next block; maybe that space would turn out to be one of those squares which dotted Paris. She decided to find out. She passed several more shuttered storefronts before reaching a traffic light, and then the seven-story rows gave way to a spectacular stretch of greenery on both sides of her. A white sign affixed to the nearest lamp post told her this was Boulevard Pereire. Rue Laugier cut through it between two sections of park enclosed by black iron fencing and gates. She looked both ways before crossing the road and then aimed for the closer of the areas. An unlocked bicycle leaned against the railing on the right, propped up on the fence's concrete base. People were scattered here and there like rose petals at season's end.

Beyond the gate, through manicured shrubs and flowering bushes, an artificial bouquet of red, blue and yellow sprang out at her: a playground. Following the squeals and shouts of children, she entered the park and determined the source of their delight. A boy and girl chased each other up ladders and across platforms; each time they propelled themselves down the larger canary-coloured slide, a woman who Michele took to be their mother reached out with a tickle, setting off a fresh round of shrieks as they began the circuit again. It was not Rutledge Park, but it pulled her in. She didn't dare sit on any of the equipment—maybe she would return after dark, when it wasn't in use—so she chose one of the nearby green benches. She wondered about this small family; what was their story? Maybe *Madame* was a stay-at-home parent who walked her well-dressed youngsters to school every morning and met them again at the end of the day after going to the market. She was married, of course, and *Monsieur* made a substantial living in the corporate world. On weekends they participated in cultural activities or went to the countryside. Maybe they had just returned from their annual vacation and were enjoying the quiet before returning to work and responsibilities.

Michele got the impression that it wasn't a tourist neighbourhood. She liked it already and wanted to know more. After consulting her brochures but not coming across any mention of Pereire, she pushed up from the bench and continued along the Promenade, reading every sign along the way until she came across what she'd been hoping for: an interpretive panel. She planted herself as firmly as the boulevard trees and drank in every word of history to quench her thirst. According to the sign, the street and the park took their name from the Pereire brothers Émile and Isaac, prominent businessmen in the nineteenth century.

"Let's see." Michele translated in her head as she went. *They founded a rail line which opened in 1854 and the park was built over that original line after it closed in 1985. Wait, hold on a sec.* A sentence struck her and she reread it twice. *The Pereire brothers created a bank, Crédit Mobilier, which was one of the world's most important financial institutions.* She blinked, dumbfounded. It was an eerie parallel with the Bouchard's and a very tangible reminder of the real reason she was in Paris.

She leaned in farther to read the rest of the text and was busy memorizing facts when an accented male voice directly behind her right shoulder pronounced, "I did not realize that your research would bring you to my neighbourhood."

Michele swivelled around to find Sébastien—in her opinion overdressed in slim navy-blue pants and a salmon dress shirt. His expression appeared serious but was punctuated by a slight smirk at the corner of his delicate mouth. Her own mouth hung open. She hadn't expected their paths to cross again, but now that he was right in front of her, she caught herself not entirely disappointed that they had. "Uh, hi! *Bonjour*. What are you doing here?"

"Well, I *do* live in Paris, if you recall," he answered. "Actually, not very far from here. I am anxious to get back to work but the law office is still closed for a few days more. So," he inserted a dramatic pause, "I have no choice but to find other ways to occupy my time."

She raised her eyebrows. "So, not to be rude, but that seems like a good problem to have. At home I hardly get a break. You should be happy to have a few days off from responsibilities."

"My job is my life. Sometimes too much, perhaps." A rogue cloud passed overhead and cast a shadow across Sébastien's face before floating away. "But, you! You must see the highlights of the city. I know that you are doing the research this week, but surely you can take some vacation time also?" Seeing her hesitate, he pressed on. "You said yourself that you are too busy in Victoria. Enjoy this time now, while you can."

"I suppose you're right. I could do some reading tonight, make some notes, and put together an itinerary that I could follow in the late afternoons and evenings after I've finished for the day." Michele shuffled through the brochures Maxine had provided, but Sébastien snatched them from her hand.

"Of course I am right. But this is not the way to do it." He tossed the pamphlets into a wrought iron garbage can before she knew what was happening.

"Hey! What did you do that for?" *Ugh, now I do wish that he'd stayed a blip in my trip memories.* She contemplated retrieving the papers but gave up when she couldn't identify most of the other contents at the bottom of the bin. There was no way she was diving in without knowing exactly what she was jumping into. She turned on Sébastien. "I needed those!"

He shook his head. "One does not get to know the real Paris through a guidebook. You have to live it firsthand."

This guy is crazy. "And how am I supposed to do that, exactly?"

He rubbed his smooth chin. "*A deux mains*. With both hands. And ears. You feel it and you hear it. You understand what I am saying?"

She was as perplexed as ever. "No. No idea."

"Let me try again. Being in Paris—truly experiencing it—is like—playing an instrument. You feel, and you listen, and eventually you make the music." Sébastien's face reddened and Michele wondered if the heat was getting to him.

She softened her tone. "Listen, I appreciate the sentiment. I get it: go out there and just explore. I'll see what I can do. But maybe you need to take your own advice? You'll be back to the 'exciting' world of law soon enough." Worried she had stuck her nose too far into his business, she added, "But that's just my observation. You do whatever you want." She lifted her shoulders and adjusted her backpack; maybe this was the opportune moment to move along.

"Not as much as you might think," Sébastien scoffed, his skin colour transitioning back to its regular shade. He picked a microscopic piece of lint from his shirt and then leaned back against a tree, crossing one leg in front of the other.

He really was a strange mix, she decided. *Just like some of those shops I saw earlier. I guess it really is a French thing.* "Well, anyway. I should get going. Nice to see you again." She spun on her heel and took off in the opposite direction.

"Wait! Michele!" he shouted behind her. She turned back and he was silhouetted against the bright sky, beams of light radiating around him as if he were an alien or an angel, (she wasn't sure which).

He caught up to her with no effort. "You may have a point," he admitted, before revising his statement. "Actually, we were both right."

"Um, we were? About what?" she muttered. "I'm pretty sure you throwing out my stuff was wrong."

He laughed. "About Paris, naturally. Wait here. I will be back in an instant." Before she could answer, he had vanished around the corner.

"OK, that was weird." Where could he possibly be going, and why should she bother to wait? She reminded herself that she had plenty to do without getting mixed up with this stranger—even if he was cute—just a little bit. "I should just go back to my room and get organized instead of wasting my time here." She went back the way she had come, skirting the rainbow playground and then slipping through the gate. As she closed it behind her, the putter of an engine filled her ears. Was that a lawnmower? She hadn't noticed the semicircular area to her right on her way in. A motorcycle was parked on the far side of it and a bicycle had found a place against this section of railing, paralleling the one she'd spotted earlier. Idling in the closest part of the curve was a mint-green scooter with a brown leather seat. The driver waiting adjacent wore a beige helmet and under his arm a matching one hung like a full moon. Michele recognized his outfit. She followed the path of blue and pink directly to Sébastien's crescent smile. "What on earth do you think you're doing?" she demanded.

He opened his arms wide, holding the passenger helmet by the chin strap with his now-outstretched hand. "We are going to—how shall I say it?—keep one another accountable, follow the other's recommendation. You will receive a genuine Paris experience, and I will have a reprieve from business matters and other preoccupations while acting as your local tour guide. Now come! We must begin your education."

She eyed the scooter. "On that? There's no way I'm getting on that thing!" This was not part of the plan—not that she entirely had one. She was on a mission and she had work to do.

"I will keep you safe, I promise it." Sébastien reached out a hand, ever so slowly, towards hers, as if he were trying to coax an injured animal out of hiding and avoiding any sudden moves so as not to frighten it. He entwined his fingers gently but firmly around hers and led her to the Vespa. "I will bring you back whenever you choose, as long as you agree to give it a chance. Please."

"OK, OK. Fine." She took a deep breath. "But just a few highlights, alright? And then straight back here."

Her "teacher" pumped his fist once in victory and handed Michele her helmet. "Put this on," he ordered before taking his place at the front of the seat. She obeyed and then struggled to swing her leg over the back. After locating the foot pegs, she searched in vain for something to hold on to; the only bar was attached to the back of the seat. *Well that's not very helpful,* she thought. *Where am I supposed to put my hands? There have to be handles, right?*

Sébastien revved the engine and turned his head over his shoulder. "You may find that we drive a little bit differently here than where you are from, so I suggest that you hold on. *Allons-y!*" With that, he abruptly turned to exit the parking area and launched their ride onto the road like a rocket. Michele's arms shot forward, locking onto his waist to keep her from falling back to Earth.

They buzzed along Boulevard Pereire until they reached a roundabout. He turned right and took them on a full rotation, pointing out the Métro station and his favourite café as cars passed what she thought was dangerously close to them. She nodded nervously and held on as tightly as possible. Soon they were back where they had started at the Promenade. Swerving at the first right, he accelerated along Avenue Niel and she yelled into his left ear, "This is a bit terrifying! I can't look." She squeezed her eyes shut and her sense of smell intensified; her nostrils puckered at the chemical blend of grease and exhaust around them with notes of cigarette smoke and urine: the less-frequently advertised smells of Paris. The Vespa stopped and started a couple of times and she assumed that it was for traffic lights although she never opened her eyes to confirm. Wherever they were, the air around them had shifted to become more charged, a restless sea in motion.

Sébastien patted her leg twice. "Michele, you cannot see Paris with your eyes closed, and I think you will like this view."

Her eyelashes lifted like a lace veil, revealing the impressive Arc de Triomphe set in a roundabout so large it made the previous one seem insignificant. For a moment the scene froze tableau-style before her. "Wow. Sébastien, it's incredible. Thank you."

He gave her an impish smile over his shoulder and replied, "This is only the first site on my list. Shall we continue?"

"OK, I guess a few more wouldn't hurt," she agreed. "But—"

"That's all I needed to hear!" He sped up and steered the scooter into the multi-lane traffic circle surrounding the famous attraction. A mad mix of taxis, tour buses, cars, cube trucks, and motorcycles engulfed them in a whirlwind of wheels and metal amongst the unmarked lanes.

She tightened her grip, her skin stretched taut and white across two rows of bony knuckles. "What are you doing?!" She let out a scream as the Vespa wove between vehicles. "You're going to get us killed!"

He honked at a silver hatchback and made a rude gesture. Somehow, he continued to confidently direct the scooter until they popped out onto one of the tree-lined avenues that branched from Place Charles de Gaulle. "Not true. I made a promise and I intend to keep it."

Why did I agree to this? Michele reprimanded herself. But her question was quickly forgotten as they zipped across the city. She was thoroughly lost for the next few hours as he drove them in all directions—at least, she guessed that it was all directions; if she'd still had her trusty map, she might have had a better idea of where they were.

Even without her paper guides, however, she eventually settled into the seat and focused on what she could sense around her rather than the mode of transportation under her. Movie theatres and luxury shops like Louis Vuitton yielded to evenly spaced and perfectly pruned horse-chestnut trees. Near the Seine River, the bitter bouquet of a flower she could not identify mingled in her nose with the heady perfume worn by elegant women striding on the sidewalks. Occasionally a whiff of baking bread interrupted like a surprise but welcome guest. Sébastien looped twice around the Place de la Concorde, giving him the opportunity to explain that the hieroglyph-clad obelisk at its centre, installed there in 1833, had come from the temple at Luxor and was one of a pair. The other one had been too difficult to move at the time and had remained stalwart in Egypt. Maybe it was because she worked in history, but it saddened her to think about the monuments separated so far and for so long. When Michele spotted the glass pyramid outside the Louvre Museum a short time later, she inquired, "What's with the Egyptian theme around here?"

"It is not a theme, though France was very much involved in the early days of Egyptology as a field," Sébastien called back. "It has been quite controversial since it was installed. I was probably ten years old at the time, and I remember the outcry very well. Some people believed that it was too modern for the classic style of the Louvre—that the two did not belong together."

She pondered his explanation as they crossed the Seine along the Pont Neuf and followed the contour of the island at the heart of the city, parking close to Notre Dame in a spot that may or may not have been legal. At the plaza in front of the grand cathedral, tourists—more specifically, their food—distracted her from the rose window and elaborately decorated entryways. Visitors, ravenous from a long morning of sightseeing, stood in the open or sat on the ledges that framed short, uniform rectangles of greenery, and scarfed down baguette sandwiches, crêpes, and even fast food burgers. The greasy smell of the latter wafted and teased her.

"Um, Sébastien?" She hammered his shoulder. "I really appreciate the tour. It's been great, it has. But I'm going to have to head back to the hotel and find something to eat pretty soon. Maybe I'll just grab a burger or something." Michele drooled over a Big Mac in the crowd even though she rarely ordered McDonald's at home.

"*MacDo?*" He sounded horrified. "Not for your first lunch in

Paris! How about a picnic instead? The French invented them, you know. It will be, as you say in English, my treat."

The offer to experience an authentic Parisian picnic was too good to pass up. And not having to pay for it was a happy bonus, though she didn't want to abuse her host's generosity. "That actually sounds amazing. Thanks."

They mounted the Vespa and, after making stops at a market and a *boulangerie*, stopped and unloaded their meal from the seat's hidden storage. Sébastien led her through a green space that had appeared out of nowhere, a hidden oasis of calm. *The parks are all so different here from the ones at home,* she observed. They strolled beside pristine lawns and trees whose leaves glowed with filtered sunlight; statues on pedestals monitored the path from above. At a wide open area with a large pond at its centre and a gorgeous historic building behind it, Sébastien selected three of the many matching curved chairs that furnished the public space and set out their meal on one of them.

"Please, sit." He arranged the baguette, pâté, cheese, and grapes before deftly opening the small bottle of white wine. "*Voilà*! A picnic at the Jardin de Luxembourg—Luxembourg Gardens. That is the palace over there. And do you see how the children sail the toy boats in the water? It is a long tradition. Eh, but now I speak too much and you are hungry. *Bon appétit.*"

Michele sampled each of the foods before her, trying her best to keep an open mind. The balance of flavours was an enjoyable surprise. But as she ate, she couldn't ignore the kids pushing their vintage wooden sailboats in the pond. They giggled as they directed the vessels with long sticks, the brightly coloured sails a bold contrast to the murky green water below. Henry would've begged to get a little boat if he were there. He would be right in the thick of things, making friends and grinning from ear to ear as he put one of his action figures inside. Batman would become a captain, crossing the sea and singing shanties along with his mates. She imagined it all playing out in front of her and then hung her head. She had been gone a whole day (or was it two with the time change?), and her son hadn't crossed her mind once. Absently biting through a piece of baguette crust, she justified the oversight to herself. *Remember, I am here for a reason, a really important reason that directly relates to my family. To Henry's family. And to accomplish this, I need to be away for a while. I will make it up to him later. But since I'm here, I think I also deserve to finally have some fun. Something just for me ...*

"*À quoi penses-tu?* What is on your mind, Michele?" Sébastien interrupted her thoughts. "You have gone far away." He furrowed his brow.

"Oh, uh, I'm sorry. Maybe I'm just a little bit homesick, you know? Adjusting to being in a new, faraway place."

He seemed crestfallen. "I am failing as your tour guide. My one job is to provide you with an enjoyable excursion. A pleasant distraction. Or," he added with a wink, "to be one."

His last comment caught her off guard and she blushed. "It's fine. You are—I mean—you did. It's been a lovely day so far. I guess my emotions are just up and down lately."

Sébastien's face perked up. Though Michele had spent only a few hours with him, she recognized by now when he was formulating one of his schemes. She could practically see the wheels turning in his head as an idea gained steam.

"Up and down.... Yes. I think I have the solution!" His emerald eyes twinkled in the afternoon sun.

Rather than her usual instinct to make excuses, Michele chuckled. "Where are you dragging me to *this* time, might I ask?" Her curiosity had gotten the better of her.

"Ah, wait and see, *ma petite*. Patience!"

They packed up the remnants of lunch, Michele licking the remains of creamy soft cheese from her fingertips and Sébastien popping a renegade grape into his mouth. They left the park behind. After reloading the scooter, they climbed on and coasted for only a few minutes, once again crossing the Seine and arriving at the Place de la Concorde.

"What are we doing back here?" she asked.

He pointed to a huge Ferris wheel that rose taller than the obelisk. "I told you, we are going up and down."

"What? No!" she protested, albeit half-heartedly, and they sauntered towards the silver ring sitting up against a Tiffany-blue sky. He paid the attendant and minutes later they had one of the open-air buckets to themselves. Before they had even left the ground, she stuck her arms out from her sides and grasped the handrail that ran along the outside. *Safety first, right?* The pod jerked up part way so that others could be filled and then lurched back and forth while it waited. The colour drained from her face. This was a lot higher than the one at the Saanich Fair and they weren't even near the top yet.

"Sébastien? I don't think I can do this," she croaked. She sat as tall and unmoving as the statues in the Luxembourg Gardens.

Her unease was obvious. In response, Sébastien methodically moved his bottom along the bench seating until he reached her shaking form. "I assure you that you are safe. Do you trust me?" She blinked yes. For whatever reason, she did trust him. He took hold of her cheeks in his warm hands. "Listen to me now. We are going to ascend again in a moment. Just breathe, and focus on me. You will not regret it." Time passed and stood still all at once and suddenly they were at the apex. He turned her head and before them lay the city of Paris in all its glory, landmarks and grey roofs spread out like a historical feast. His hands came down to rest on her lap and Michele squeezed them. She had never seen anything so beautiful before in her life. It was an entirely new perspective.

After three rotations their time ended. In comfortable silence, they rode the Vespa away from the core to a part of town they had not yet visited. As they bounced up and down narrow cobbled streets in the hills of what Sébastien informed her was the Montmartre district, the enticing scent of freshly grilled steaks floated to them from café terraces. "This area was very popular with artists," he said, reverting to tour guide mode. "Many famous painters lived and worked here." He took her to the domed Sacré-Cœur Basilica before heading downhill. "Now for a brief change of pace, I will show you a different side of Paris." Her cheeks turned as red as the signs advertising adult shops and live theatres. The namesake windmill atop the Moulin Rouge turned while tourists took blurry photos from the street. Sébastien followed Boulevard de Clichy and then pulled into a scooter parking zone in the meridian. "Ready for a break?"

She was thankful the trees helped block her view of the suggestive stores. As an added precaution, she focused on Sébastien, who bounced along the walkway making funny faces. His giddiness was infectious and before long she joined in, twirling in full view of sketchy passers-by. Spontaneously he took her hand, lightly held her waist, and led her in a dance. It made her tipsy, but happy, like drinking a glass of wine. He hummed, and the hum evolved into singing. The lyrics to "Michelle" shocked her ears and sent her into an uncontrollable spin. *No, please stop. Anything but that.*

Delirious, she separated herself from him and stumbled into the street, a wild creature fleeing into the jungle. "I'm sorry, I can't—" She jumped around an oncoming car, teetered across the road, and desperately searched for something familiar to ground her. Golden Arches. McDonald's. It would have to do. She ran inside and straight to the women's single bathroom, locking the door and sliding down along it until she landed on the grimy floor. *Breathe, breathe. Find three things. Slow down.* Her heart rate abated and the room stopped moving, permitting rational thought. "Oh gosh, Sébastien's going to think I'm a nutcase. I have to go talk to him—if he hasn't bolted, that is." Michele stood up and made use of the toilet before washing her hands; it gave her another minute to collect herself. Exhaling, she pulled the door, but it remained shut. She tried the knob again and rattled it hard, feeling a rising panic. The latch must have jammed. *No!* She was in a fast food restaurant bathroom in the Red-Light District of Paris and she was locked in.

CHAPTER 7

Today a knock came at the door. <u>The</u> knock. The knock that too many of my friends and neighbours have received and that I had prayed would never reach me. It was a telegraph boy, delivering a notice stating that Philippe is missing over Normandy and presumed dead. How ironic that the place where he was born, the fields that could not contain him, should be the place where he falls. There are certain connections from which one cannot separate oneself, no matter how hard he tries—if he is even aware of them at all. The roots are there regardless, and pull even the highest branches in profound and subtle ways.

I wait now to see where my own origins will take me, if an ancestor will have passed on some of her fortitude and faith. How many young women became brides, mothers and widows within the span of a few short years and endured? I do not know the answer. But because today I cannot bear to look forward, I turn for comfort to the past.

* * *

Wednesday, August 19, 2009

What do I do now? Should I scream for help? Shaking the door hadn't gotten her anywhere and Michele's fists had tired of banging against it in vain, but she had to get out. No one knew where she was and Sébastien was probably long gone, so she had only herself to rely on. It was just as well. She forced herself to stand still, closed her eyes, and did nothing for a full minute. With a renewed air of calm, she tried the lock again, jiggling it with far less vigour. And just like that, a small click. She was free! She straightened her shirt, smoothed her disorderly hair back into place, and strode out of the bathroom with her chin held artificially high. Her crimson face must have given her away, but she needed to at least try to maintain some semblance of dignity. Keeping her eyes forward, she cut a path through the gawkers, left McDonalds, and caught a glimpse of the Pigalle Métro station entrance. Maybe she could find her way to the hotel if she could remember the name of the stop Sébastien had showed her. Wasn't it Pereire? It stood to reason, given that the Boulevard was directly above. She would check the subway map sign and work out the route.

She crossed the street and turned right, sights set on the Art Nouveau *METROPOLITAIN* sign above the mounted map. As she reached it, Sébastien came running to her from where she'd last seen him, the green space in the next block. He hadn't left. She cocked her head and studied him as if he were a rare bird. His face had lost its earlier exuberance and his shirt clung to his damp torso.

"Michele! What happened to you? I have been searching everywhere!" The corners of his eyes ran deeper than before and he appeared concerned. A rush of guilt surprised her. She had worried him—he had worried about her. How very odd.

"I'm so sorry. I ... didn't feel well. It came on very suddenly," she apologized. "It was super weird, and I wouldn't have blamed you if you had taken off. But," she added without thinking, "I'm glad you didn't."

At that, Sébastien lifted. "Of course. I would not leave." One half of his mouth turned up and the other followed after it. "As your guide, and I believe your only friend in Paris, I have a responsibility. You are in my charge."

"How nice of you to take pity on me," Michele joked. "But

seriously, after that—episode, I need some down time. Maybe head back to Pereire. Would you take me?"

"*Absolument.*"

* * *

A short time later, they arrived back where they had started the day only a few hours before. Sébastien parked the Vespa and opened the Promenade gate for Michele, following her into the park. As they ambled along, he snuck his hand around hers. She did not comment but didn't pull away either. Together they chose one of the green benches near the playground and watched a little girl take on a cherry red climbing structure. They sat in shared tranquility for several minutes and then Sébastien turned to Michele and asked again, "Are you sure that you are feeling alright? I could take you to a doctor."

"No, I'm much better now. Thank you." The silence settled upon them once more until she dispersed it, dandelion seeds launched into the sky with a single breath. "This park reminds me of the one behind my house in Victoria, even though they're different." He waited for her to continue. "I go there sometimes to think, you know? There's this pink concrete elephant that all the neighbourhood kids love. And actually, I love it too. It's a good spot to sit—and see things a bit more clearly."

Sébastien nodded. "I understand this. I come frequently here and to the Square Albert-Besnard inside the traffic circle, though not as often as I would like. The Law, she is a demanding mistress, and I cannot say no to her. It has caused some ... problems in my life. Sometimes I give all of my energy and my passion to my work and not other important things." Michele noted a sadness in his expression but did not press him. He shifted as if uncomfortable, but when he spoke again, his mood had improved. "Enough of the melancholy! Do you want to get a drink?"

They left the park, walked two blocks along Boulevard Pereire, and turned right at the roundabout, coming to the café Sébastien had announced at the beginning of his tour. The Royal Pereire stood out at its corner with a bold red awning, the name in neon lights, a tiara sitting on top; white chairs and tables adorned the sidewalk like a pearl necklace. They found two empty seats and then inserted themselves into the tight space, the bistro table wobbling precariously. As they sat down, she smiled politely at the moustached man perched at the table behind them in the raised interior seating. His rumpled suit hung from his body as he stooped over a plate of raw beef topped with an equally raw egg. He looked like a depressed blend of Thomas Magnum, Colombo, and Norm from Cheers. She wasn't sure if it was his cold attitude or his cold meal, but she couldn't look away fast enough.

Around them, servers roamed while customers tried without success to get their attention. The staff must have known Sébastien, however; a waiter appeared at his side and took his order, returning shortly afterwards with a bottle of wine for approval. As they sipped the floral white, she noticed that Sébastien kept looking behind him at the man she had already secretly dubbed Suit Jacket Dude.

"Do you know him?" she whispered in Sébastien's ear.

"Not personally, but he is a regular customer," he responded, avoiding eye contact.

Michele would not let him off so easily. "Then why are you watching him so much?"

Sébastien swirled the amber drink in his glass and stared through it as if it were a crystal ball revealing his turbulent future. "Do you remember in the park when I told you about my work taking the first place in my life? I have a great fear that if I continue in this way, I will end up like that sad man—alone—with only my past career accomplishments to keep me company." He kept his eyes fixed on his wine.

"What?" she said, wanting to reassure him. "I highly —*highly*— doubt you will end up like that guy. You are kind, and funny, and any woman would be lucky to be with you."

"My ex-wife would disagree."

Michele set her glass down in slow motion. "Wife? You were married?"

"I was, briefly. But Claudette accused me of having eyes only for my profession. She was right, of course. I worked all hours, focused exclusively on advancing myself." He paused to wet his lips and then finally looked her in the eye. "Michele, I moved up to a high level at the law firm, but I did some terrible things to get to this place. I helped awful people. It was shameful; something that my grandfather would do, and I do not want to be like him. I know the reality of his practices, not only the public image. But I made these choices precisely so that I could be independent from my family. I hope to open my own firm soon, but I want to do this without any help from them. Do you understand?"

Sébastien was a lot more complex than she'd realized. If it was confession time, she should probably throw in one of her own, to keep things fair. "Actually, I think I do. I work in an archives—you know, history, old documents—and I think I've finally found what I'm meant to do. But I also have a five-year-old son. It's just the two of us," she made sure to add. "And I guess I've gotten used to managing by myself. I prefer it, really." Not wanting to elaborate further, she flipped the attention back to him before he could ask any questions. "But what about your family? Would it be so bad to accept some support from them to get you started?"

"I assure you that it would. They would like nothing more than for me to give up my 'crazy' ideas and to join the family business, especially now when there are important matters under consideration. My grandfather even went so far as to offer me a position as head of the legal team." Sébastien shook his head in disbelief, or exasperation. "It is difficult to escape what he likes to grandly call the 'family legacy.' He will not be satisfied until I am working for him and living back at home."

"So that's why, at least partially, you have your own place, right? I mean, other than because you're an adult and it's normal to have your own life." *Ugh, what a stupid thing to say. OK, Michele, maybe ease up on the drinks.*

He finished the last drops of his wine, pulled some cash out of his wallet, and deposited it on the table. "My independence is very important to me. My place and this neighbourhood, they suit me very well. In fact," he got up and held out his hand, "now that we have explored the *quartier*, I would love to show you my humble dwelling. Please, allow me to make you dinner this evening. Perhaps we might watch a film first?"

Well, it's not like I'm going to be doing any research tonight anyway, she thought. *I've already spent all day with him, I might as well enjoy the evening too.* She let him lift her up out of her chair and they stole away into the late afternoon sun, leaving Suit Jacket Dude and his uncooked plate ensconced in the shadows.

* * *

Sébastien lived on the main floor of a white three-storey building on Boulevard Pereire, only two blocks from the Hotel Magellan on the opposite side of the park. The navy-blue door and the tall, rectangular windows on the first two levels were framed by elaborate moulding and scrollwork above them, and in the case of the windows, black wrought iron flower boxes underneath. Michele could not think of anything more Parisian. The mansard roof took up the entire top floor; its three smaller windows, which she noted were divided into six panes each, surveyed the park from under thick, dark dormers. She admired the brass door knocker on the way in and wondered if anyone ever used it. As far as she could see, there was no button for a bell. Inside, the space was sparse but homey. Like Sébastien, it was a mix of styles: old and new, bold and muted. A perfect, confusing blend. As she took in the tiny living room, she tried to reconcile his home with his career. For a lawyer who wore high end shoes and watches, his suite was especially simple. His living and his, well, living, didn't seem to match.

"Please, make yourself comfortable." He invited her to sit on the white apartment-sized sofa as he opened a cabinet and then rummaged inside. "Are you familiar with the American actor John Cusack? I am a very big fan of his work." He emerged with several DVDs in his hands.

"I've been into Nicholas Cage lately. I don't really know any of John Cusack's stuff. How about we just watch your favourite?"

"Ah! He is brilliant in everything, but I will show you his best film. It really is criminal to not ever have watched it, but we will remedy this now, yes? I do not want to have to turn you in." With a wink, Sébastien put the other DVDs away and came back waving the case for *High Fidelity*. He inserted the disc into the player and backed himself onto the couch beside her. "I should warn you that there is a significant amount of cursing, but do not let that turn you off."

Duly cautioned, Michele sat with the posture of a Victorian

schoolmarm as a kind of counterbalance to the foul language. As the plot unfolded, she tried to keep an open mind. *He definitely wasn't joking about the swearing.* Despite that, she had to admit that the story, with its quirky setting, was pretty fun. But when it came to the main character, Rob, her feelings were mixed. Something about the lovelorn record shop owner's commitment issues rubbed her the wrong way, but she couldn't quite put her finger on it. Was it that he was selfish? He did always seem ready to bolt. At the same time, she could kind of understand his attitude. Regardless, she did feel sorry for him as he pined for his ex-girlfriend, Laura. His list of the top five things he missed about her floated in Michele's thoughts, especially number three; some people really did feel like home. She snuck a glance at Sébastien as he snickered at a scene, then she looked back at the TV. *That's funny, Laura's a lawyer too. I wonder if that's why this is his favourite movie?*

By the time it ended, Michele had completely forgotten about posture and was slouched deep into her seat, shoulder to shoulder with Sébastien. They watched the credits roll to the end before moving. He rose first.

"And now, I must tend to our dinner. You just relax, I will take care of everything." He pulled out ingredients and pans from storage hidden in what she supposed was the kitchen. To her it was a clown car, able to hold much more than seemed humanly possible. After a few minutes of methodical chopping, he placed a dish of sliced radishes and apples on the table in front of her. "Something to prepare the palate. I promise that the entree will be worth the wait." She was unconvinced but took a piece of each and dropped them in her mouth. She was surprised to discover that the radish and apple were the freshest she'd ever tasted. Her tongue came alive under the spicy and sweet fusion. How could something so straightforward create such a complex flavour? The equilibrium was flawless. It set the stage for the main course, which arrived a short time later: grilled chicken with green beans and roasted baby potatoes. It didn't look fancy, but Sébastien served it with a flourish. "*Et voilà!*"

Michele took a bite. "This is delicious! But I don't get it. I've served this kind of food before and it tasted nothing like this." She put down her fork and crossed her arms to interrogate him. "What's your secret?"

He shrugged in that blasé way of his and speared a green bean. "It is because I am French. It cannot be helped. But I will reveal this: it is also because of the company. The dining companion is a critical element."

She blushed and poked at her chicken. Had the room gotten hotter all of a sudden? And yet she could see through the window that the sun had already gone down. She never, ever ate this late at home. Where had the hours gone?

As they completed their meal with a dessert of dense, creamy yogurt, juicy peach slices, and dark chocolate, she examined the apartment. Near the door to what she guessed was Sébastien's bedroom, a case mounted to the wall displayed a violin. The instrument appeared old but immaculately kept, and she knew immediately that it had a story. "That's a beautiful violin you have over there."

"It belonged to my great uncle. He died decades ago at a relatively young age. I have been told that I am like him in many ways, though knowing my family I am not certain if this was meant as a compliment or an insult—I choose to believe the former. Either way, perhaps this is why my mother gave the violin to me." He cleared the dishes, skillfully balancing them as he took them away.

She decided to get a closer look inside the case. "Do you play?"

she called out.

Sébastien returned from the kitchen. "Only a little. My great uncle was apparently quite talented, but unfortunately I did not inherit the same proficiency."

"Well, I would love to hear you. I promise I won't laugh or anything. Please?" she begged.

"Very well, very well." He threw up his hands. "Who am I to deny a request from the person who elevated my cooking this evening?"

Michele installed herself on the arm of the sofa while he brought out the violin and bow from their chamber. He carried the instrument to the living area and sat on the table. Bringing up the chin rest and lining his fingers along the neck, he drew the bow across the strings. She closed her eyes and absorbed the melody: quiet and uncertain at first, it gradually built up to a stirring crescendo. It enfolded her, every note dancing along her arms and legs and leaving behind a field of goosebumps. She did not know the tune, but she was sure she'd heard it somewhere before. Concentrating, she let it funnel into her ears until the music abruptly ended.

"That is all I know, I swear it," he insisted.

"No, don't stop! That was so beautiful." Her eyes snapped open like a released roller shade to let his sparkling countenance shine in. This time he did not tease or brag. She felt like she was seeing him clearly for the first time.

He returned the violin to the case, contemplative. "Thank you. It has been a very long time since I have played. Perhaps I will take up practicing once again. Will that suffice for now?"

"Alright, fine. But I'm going to hold you to that."

"It is, as you say, a deal. Now, before we were distracted by the music, I did have another activity in mind to conclude the evening.

Are you too tired, or can you handle one more adventure tonight?"

Michele didn't hesitate. "I'm in."

* * *

"No tour of the City of Lights is complete without seeing it at night," Sébastien informed her as they climbed on the Vespa. Unlike that morning, this time she locked her arms around her driver and guide not by reflex but on purpose. The route was the same—at least she thought it was. With this second chance, she chose to keep her eyes open so she wouldn't miss a single thing. He turned onto Place Charles de Gaulle and she hollered "Woo hoo!" as they rode beside the Arc de Triomphe, glorious as if it had been gilded by magic after nightfall. They circled it three times and then exited to the Champs-Élysées. The rows of trees so prominent in the daytime had receded into the background, replaced by lights lining both sides of the street like a runway. At a massive ornate building, he took a right and slowed down. "Do you see that bronze statue on top?"

"It's kind of hard not to! Those horses are so animated, especially lit up like that. Who are the other figures supposed to be, though?" She pointed out a woman with a laurel dominating the sculpture on top and an old bearded man sitting below the four rearing animals.

"Ah, she is Immortality, standing victorious over Time. This is always the human desire, *non*? To be remembered long after we have left this world. This is how we can live for eternity."

"I feel like that's what archives do. When I hold and read old documents, it's like the people inside them, the people who created them, are still alive." *People like my grandmother,* she added silently.

They followed traffic to an extravagant bridge where golden winged horses high atop carved stone pillars marked the entrance.

Black Art Nouveau lamps along the deck guided pedestrians the length of the ultra-wide sidewalk. Sébastien pointed to the right, and there across the water the Eiffel Tower glittered like a constellation. He pulled over to the curb, ignoring a car horn behind him. "This is said to be the most beautiful bridge in Paris. *Qu'en penses-tu?* What do you think?"

Michele had trouble getting her tongue to work. "I think it's incredible. Better than I ever could have imagined. I can confidently say that nothing could possibly top this."

He raised his eyebrows. "Nothing? Hmm, I accept your challenge. The night is not over yet!"

Minutes later, he had tucked his scooter into a dark corner and brought her to the base of one of the Eiffel Tower's elegant iron legs. The lattice metalwork arched and stretched to the sky, the tall landmark showing off her figure to the world. Assuming they were heading to the top, Michele frowned at the long line up. "Looks like it's going to be a while."

"*Alors*, in that case it is good that it is not our destination."

"It is? I mean, it's not?"

"*Non.* Come, I will show you." They crossed the street and came to a classic carousel. The scalloped top and gingerbread trim glowed, the lonely white wooden horses inside awaiting their next riders. He paid the bored operator and then guided her up the steps onto the platform. A vision sprang into her mind of Prince Charming helping Cinderella into her carriage, but she chased it away. This was not a fairy tale, just a ride for children—nothing more. They picked two horses side by side and climbed onto their backs. The carousel began to spin, picking up speed as French accordion music played. Up and down the mounts galloped—Michele's ahead of Sébastien's—and gears and bodies waltzed as the platform rotated. She studied the scenes on the painted ceiling, the primary colours decorating her horse's sides, the crowd back at the tower.

"Michele." Sébastien extended his arm and grazed her chin with his fingertips. The yellow bulbs around them glowed brighter as a power surge passed through.

Hypnotized by the electricity, she moved towards him. Their faces drew closer and closer to each other as the horses, coming from opposite directions, neared the same height.

"Sébastien ..." she answered. Just as she closed her eyes, however, the ride slowed down, signalling the end. He cleared his throat and dismounted while the carousel completed its last turn. She stared ahead, her back as straight as the pole she gripped.

As they hiked to the Vespa, his body language became resolute and he asked without warning, "So, may I meet you at the park tomorrow morning at nine o'clock? I will give you my mobile number in case you need to reach me."

"Yes, it's a date." She was ready to count down every hour until it arrived.

* * *

Thursday, August 20, 2009

At ten minutes to nine, Michele bounded down the stairs inside the Hotel Magellan. Maxine, who had just finished assisting another guest, greeted her with a friendly *bonjour.* "Are you off to work on your project?" she asked.

"What? Oh, that. I have some other plans first." It was Michele's second full day in Paris and Maxine's question had reminded her that she had not even started what she'd come to do yet. "Good thing I have a whole week here, I guess." Her voice trailed off. After vowing to make the most of the morning so she could get to work in the afternoon, she said goodbye to the front desk agent and dashed out the door. She skipped past the buildings along the way rather than studying every detail, simply noting them as part of the landscape. In her haste to get to the park on time, she did not once ask herself about their history.

Sébastien was waiting on his Vespa at the gate outside the playground. "You are very punctual—I appreciate this. Many French women, they arrive always late to make the entrance. It is expected."

"So, you could say that I'm unexpected?" Michele teased.

"Very much, but pleasantly so." He moved to allow her on the scooter and then indulged in a dramatic pause. "And now, our outing awaits. *C'est parti.* We are off."

He drove northeast, following Boulevard Pereire past the roundabout. The road curved and then paralleled multiple rail lines on their left for a time. Eventually, the tracks were lost from view behind, or perhaps under, the classic apartment blocks. He carried on past a columned structure that looked like a Greek temple. "That is L'église de la Madeleine, a Catholic Church." Michele would have to tell Mrs. Eliades about it; maybe she had seen similar buildings back home in Greece. After veering to the right, he sped up only to take two lefts in quick succession and then proceeded into an open square of uniform architecture. The consistency of the design was pleasing to the eye. "And here is Place Vendôme, known for its high-end jewellery shops. The Hôtel Ritz is in the far corner, over there. Ironically, the first two owners of the *Place* had to give it up because of a lack of funds." He leaned into the curves of the oval street and Michele tried to figure out what the hurry was. The square was lovely, and the threaded, sea-green column at its centre made her think of the carousel poles. She tightened her grip on him as they looped through and left. They circumvented the Place de la Concorde a few minutes later and headed towards the Seine River. In fact, he drove as near to it as possible and parked in front of a glass and concrete building on the water. "This is it," he proclaimed.

Michele scratched her head. "*What* is it? What are we doing?"

"*We*," Sébastien emphasized as he stowed the helmets, "are taking a cruise. We have seen the city from high and low, during the day and at night, by land—and now—by water. This will round out your education. For the next hour, we shall see the sights of the Left and Right Banks from the comfort of a Bateau-Mouche. I took the liberty of making the reservation in advance."

"That sounds fantastic! Let's do it."

They didn't have to wait long to board. Once they had been cleared to proceed, Michele and Sébastien took the stairs to the top deck. The vessel, which she could see from the stern was named *L'espoir*—Hope—easily accommodated hundreds of passengers. Row after row of tangerine chairs filled the open-air upper level like fruit packed on a tree. She picked two seats at the back, away from the tourists pushing forward for a better view, and slid in, followed closely by Sébastien. When the boat moved away from the dock and the commentary commenced through the speakers, however, all she really wanted to know about was the person beside her. "So, you didn't have anything more important to do today? Like maybe go see your family?"

"I am sure that they are very busy. My grandfather does not believe in *les vacances*." Sébastien crossed his right ankle over his left thigh and laced his fingers behind his head. "It is possible that *Maman* is out shopping. I would not be surprised if she was in one of the luxury stores in Place Vendôme. She is a frequent customer, which causes some friction since grandfather detests wasteful spending. To be honest with you, I was worried that we might see her earlier. Despite her habits, however, she is smart when it comes to business. She is very much my grandfather's daughter."

"Sounds complicated. But I think most families are. Do you get along with them at all?"

Sébastien took his time before answering. "We love each other very much, in our own ways. I know that I have been complaining about them to you, but *en fin de compte*, they are my family. And they have done some noble work, even if only for public recognition. I must give the credit where credit is due. They are infuriating and we argue more often than not, but loyalty is everything to us."

"That's not a bad thing. You said your grandfather was trying to get you to work for him, right? Do you think you ever would?"

"Not unless it was absolutely necessary. I respect him, but I am not crazy!" He chuckled before turning the tables on her. "Tell me about this family research that you travelled all this way to do."

Michele yielded to his request. It might help her to talk about it out loud, and she found herself wanting to share with him. "It's definitely complicated, but here's the short version. I found a diary— written in French—and it turns out it was my grandmother's. She was from France but eventually immigrated to Victoria. She married a Frenchman and they had a daughter, my mother. My grandfather was killed overseas—here, I mean—in the Second World War and my grandmother later fell in love again with this amazing man who coincidentally was also French." She felt her cheeks go red but carried on. "They were going to get married and spend the rest of their lives together, but unfortunately he died suddenly. What she hadn't known was that he was actually quite wealthy back home. My grandmother was a single mom, like me, and she could have really used some financial support. She writes in her diary that her fiancée wanted to make sure she and her daughter were looked after. But his family, who controlled everything, had other ideas and she was left with nothing. She couldn't fight it because, one, she couldn't afford to, and two, they weren't married yet when he died. My mother never dug herself out of that poverty, and my parents gave me up when I was young because of it, in part. So anyway, I came here to track the man's family down and confront them. Go public if necessary." Michele stopped to catch her breath. "Now that I'm saying it out loud, it sounds insane. But I want to ask them how they could have been so cruel." She watched the Paris scenery scroll by. "I never knew any of them, you know. I grew up with my best friend and her parents, who adopted me. So this is kind of a big deal."

She felt Sébastien take hold of her hand, which had contracted into a fist during her exposition. He brushed her hair back from her face, encouraging her to turn with it and to him. His visage was an Impressionist painting, a thousand brushstrokes of sympathy and caring and something more.

"It is the very biggest 'deal.' Why did you not say something earlier? I have kept you from this most important mission."

"It's OK, really. This—" She brought her other hand around to meet the ones that had already joined. "—this has been incredible."

"I agree." With Notre Dame in the background they kissed, shyly at first and then explosively. Flocks of pigeons at the cathedral flew into the sky, grey fireworks shooting up, up to their highest point and then forming a circle above Sébastien and Michele before dispersing. On the boat, limbs and hair and clothing criss-crossed in a frenzied display until the air cleared. He draped his arm around her shoulders, and she pressed her head into his chest. As she drew figure-eights on his dress shirt, his steady voice floated down to her. "I want to aid you in your search. Family is so important. Maybe there is some way that I can help."

Search. Family. Help. She tensed up. The smooth surface of the boat deck under her feet, Sébastien's aromatic cologne with hints of forest and spice, the pergola of stone bridges above them—it was all too much. *What am I doing here?* In all the fun and frivolity, her responsibilities had clearly gone out the window. She pulled away from him and pressed the heels of her hands hard into her eye sockets. "I'm a terrible person!"

"What are you talking about, *ma petite?*"

"No. No *'petite.'* No to all of this. I've gotten way off track here. I need to call my son, right now. Please take me back to the hotel as soon as we dock." She looked Sébastien in his hurt eyes. "Please."

* * *

"Isn't it the middle of the night there?" Sébastien stood in the hotel hallway just outside Michele's open door while she dialled from the room phone. Hearing ringing, she shushed him.

On the other end a small, sleepy voice finally answered. "Mummy, is that you?"

"Henry? Yes, it's me! How are you? I'm so sorry I haven't called," she blubbered. "Wait, you're not tall enough to reach the phone."

"I pushed a chair from the kitchen. I had to run really fast down the stairs too, but that's OK because I knew it was you and I miss you."

She wiped away a tear. "I miss you too, Henry. I'm really sorry for waking you up. I just needed to hear your voice." She caught Sébastien's eye and smiled.

"OK. Oh, hold on, Didi just came out and she wants to talk too. Goodnight, Mummy!"

A second later the unmistakably deep intonation of Mrs. Eliades assaulted her ear. "Michele, you phoning at two o'clock in the morning, and you wake up the boy and me too? I tell you right now, somebody better have died for you to be calling me." The volume was loud enough that Sébastien mouthed, "Is everything alright?"

Oh gosh, this was a mistake. Shoot, shoot, shoot. She wasn't as understanding as John. *Think fast, Michele.* "Please forgive me, I wasn't thinking straight. It's just that I hadn't been in contact at all yet—"

"I noticed. And so. Did. Your. Son," Mrs. Eliades emphasized every syllable.

"I know. It's been busy here—"

"And this emergency? Is OK now? How soon you come home?"

"The thing is ... the *truth* is, that I recently learned who my parents and my grandparents are. I didn't know them, but I'm trying to now, for my sake and Henry's, too. And I found out that someone here in Paris did them wrong. Not just wrong, a huge injustice, and it changed everything." The receiver trembled in Michele's hand. "I need to make it right." In the hallway, Sébastien nodded his support.

"What are you saying? This sounds like a game or something strange. You need to come home, and then you need to pay the rent." Mrs. Eliades lowered her voice. "Or move out."

Michele paled and looked away from Sébastien before butting her mouth against the handset. "OK, I hear you. Listen, as soon as I track down the Bouchard's, I'll head home, alright? I promise." She thought she heard a gasp as she hung up but couldn't be sure between the static and the noises in the hotel. *At least that's over with. Now to finally do what I came here for.* "Sébastien, I've been thinking, and maybe you can help after all. Could you give me a ride to—" She pivoted back to find an empty doorway. He was gone.

CHAPTER 8

February 2, 1944

We must, each of us, do what is necessary in the war effort, just as our loyal boys do overseas. It is difficult with an infant, but I contribute where I am able. Twice a week I make the trip to Government Street to the Salvation Army canteen and serve apple pie to the hungry soldiers. In the Colonist I have read advertisements to do salvage work. I am not sure that I qualify, but if I can arrange it, then I too will "work for victory."

The feeling of fear dwells everywhere. At home, I knit and stitch and listen for news on the radio. Aircraft seem to be constantly screaming from over nearby Cordova Bay, and my mind travels to Philippe: manning the guns in a plane halfway across the world in a battle into which he flew headlong and strong. He never paused long enough to be afraid. To be effective here, I must also control my emotions, and this I do by keeping busy. Now is not the time for idle hands.

* * *

Thursday, August 20, 2009

"Sébastien?" Michele stuck her head out the door and checked up and down the hallway. "That's really weird. Where did he go?" Puzzled, she returned inside. Thinking he might have come in to use the bathroom, she had a look to make sure but he wasn't there. *It's not like this is a huge room or anything. There aren't exactly a lot of places he could be,* she thought. Which meant he had gone. The question was, why? He had told her at Pigalle that he wouldn't leave her, right? And he seemed to take the whole "tour guide" role pretty seriously.

Then again, she had messed up the river cruise experience royally. They had kissed, and what had she done? A complete one-eighty. Maybe he had only brought her back to the hotel because she had asked him to and because he was a gentleman. Had he just been waiting for an opportunity to sneak away? *No, that doesn't add up. I know him, and he wouldn't do that,* she told herself. *At least, I don't think he would.* She analyzed how much she actually knew about him. He was a lawyer and a Parisian who lived in the Pereire neighbourhood. He had a complicated relationship with his overbearing family. He was a little arrogant, but charming overall. He played the violin well and kissed even better ...

No, something terrible must have happened. What if there had been an emergency with his grandfather or mother or another one of his relatives? She hadn't heard his mobile ring, but she had been busy on her own call. There was no way Sébastien would abandon his family if they needed him. It was just the type of person he was—of that she had no doubt. She reminisced about all the times he had been there for her since they had run into each other at the park yesterday. He was—what had he called her? Unexpected. A terrifying possibility came to her mind. What if Sébastien was the one who was in some kind of trouble? He appeared healthy, but what if he'd been struck by some kind of medical issue? If he needed urgent care, he still might not seek it out. Yesterday he had worried about her during her attack; now it was her turn to be concerned. She had to find him.

She grabbed her backpack and ran out the door, slamming it in her rush to leave. *OK, think. Where would he go?* After blowing past Maxine at the front desk to the street, Michele sprinted along Rue Jean-Baptiste Dumas and Rue Laugier, past the Promenade, and left onto Boulevard Pereire. She hadn't seen Sébastien's scooter in front of the hotel or anywhere along the way; she just hoped he had been well enough to drive it safely. It was quiet outside his apartment when she arrived. She went up to the window and cupped her hands to the glass. The couch where they had watched *High Fidelity* only the night before was empty, as was the table where they had enjoyed his fabulous dinner. She couldn't see the bedroom or the bathroom since they were around the corner—the violin display case was well out of sight—but she got the distinct impression he was not home.

"So much for that," she whispered. If he'd been there, at least she would know he was alright. She rested against the white wall and dreamed of rewinding to last evening when he had played the violin. He may have been uncharacteristically humble about his skill, but she could tell the music came naturally to him. Funny, she could almost hear it now.

Compiling a mental list of the other places he frequented, she aimed next for the Promenade. The lone child on the playground jumped down from a spring rocker and ran off, leaving the blue dolphin tottering on its own. The place was deserted. Michele jogged down the walkway a couple of blocks and then back again, scouring the green benches on top and underneath and circling every tree. It was a reach—he likely wasn't hiding in the shrubbery—but she didn't know what else to do but be thorough. Besides, if he *had* passed out, then he *could* be under a bench or behind a bush. She couldn't risk missing him; she had to investigate every possibility.

As she left the park, she scanned the parking area at the end and found only two motorcycles. A translucent image of Sébastien's green Vespa formed in front of her, taking her back to the first time she had seen his scooter. Had that really been only a day and a half ago? It was hard for her to believe she'd ever been apprehensive about climbing on. Just before he had taken off, she'd been about to ask him to drive her to the Bouchard Financial offices. She needed to go there regardless, but she would have used any excuse to ride with him again. She marvelled at how much had changed in such a short time.

Next, she ran to the roundabout and to the Royale Pereire. She paced the sidewalk, patrolling the chairs lined up outside the café. A strain of mournful music playing somewhere in the distance was lost under the cheerier tunes from the bistro's speakers. The sun was nearly at its apex, and she tried to hide the dark patches growing under her arms as she scrutinized the faces visible from the street. It was too early for lunch, for the French at least, but well past breakfast so only a few patrons populated the tables. She didn't see Sébastien but did recognize one person.

At his regular table, Suit Jacket Dude contemplated his coffee—or perhaps something stronger. It looked like he had not moved since the day before; his grey suit still drooped down his stooped shoulders, the wrinkles in the fabric matching those around his features. *I wonder what made him this way. And how could Sébastien ever think he would become like this guy?* Yes, Sébastien was dedicated to his work and probably needed to learn to take a step back. And yes, he had said he'd done some sketchy things in his career to get ahead, but how bad could they have been? From what Michele had deduced, his grandfather and his mother could be brutal when it came to business, but he was nothing like them—not based on what she had seen and heard for herself, anyway.

Giving the café a last once-over, she was about to concede defeat when a waiter met her. "Oh, *bonjour*," she stammered. Somewhere she had read that French etiquette demanded a salutation first, especially in a shop or restaurant.

"*Table pour une personne?* Table for one?" he asked.

She identified him as the one who had served them before. At the time he had seemed familiar with Sébastien, so she decided to try her luck. In her best French she explained, "I was here yesterday afternoon with my ... friend, and now I'm looking for him." She steered the waiter to the same terrace table to jog his memory. "I think he comes here often, so maybe you know him? His name is Sébastien."

"*Ah, oui. Bien sûr.* Of course. *Monsieur* Lechavalier. He is a valued customer. But he has not come in today."

Lechevalier. At least now I have his last name. But as far as leads, she still had no idea where he had gone and she'd exhausted the options on her initial list. Time to regroup and recharge. "May I take this table after all? I will get some food, and with any luck he will show up while I eat."

"*Très bien, Mademoiselle.*" The waiter took her order and withdrew inside, leaving her with her thoughts. Sébastien had *not* been part of the plan, and plans were essential. But this time she had not even followed the one she'd had in the first place. Now she was no closer to closure for her family; she had only known about them for a few days and had already screwed it up. Maybe she should drop the whole thing and go home. She had no shortage of her own problems to deal with back in Victoria. What good was coming to Paris on this wild goose chase if she and Henry wound up homeless at the end of it all? Michele put an elbow on the table and propped her chin on her hand until the waiter returned with sparkling water and a plate of fries. The taste of crispy, salty potatoes, like everything bagels, was comfortable and reassuring. Plus, they were the cheapest option on the menu. A sensible choice.

As she dubiously dipped the *frites* in the mayonnaise that came on the side, Michele jumped back to Sébastien. Being with him felt so natural—she couldn't deny it. What if they had been meant to meet all along? Was that even possible? She had never taken the concept of destiny seriously, but her time in Paris so far had mixed everything up in her head. With him, plans seemed inconsequential. The days filled themselves organically and organizing them ahead of time was, incredibly, no longer needed. It was hard to explain to herself, let alone anyone else.

Amanda will think I've lost my mind if I tell her about any of this. She certainly didn't give me a trip to Paris so I could live out some romantic fantasy. She polished off the last of the *frites* and dabbed her mouth with a napkin. Was that what this whirlwind with Sébastien was—a romance? It was hard to know for sure when she didn't have anything to compare it to. The only thing she was certain of was that she did not want it to end.

She left the café and hurried back to the hotel. Maybe there was a way to reach him after all. Skipping steps, she climbed to her floor and then fumbled to dig the key card out of her backpack. In the hallway a couple, obviously getting a late start to the day, tumbled out of their room with tousled hair and passed her arm in arm. *At least* someone *has got the romance of Paris down pat,* she quipped to herself. When at last she had gained entry, she zipped to the desk and rifled through the papers on top. Bingo! The fragment on which Sébastien had scribbled his number stuck out from under a hotel information sheet. She could not have cared less about checkout time or how to request an extra pillow; the only number that interested her was his. Michele called his cell phone, anxious. "Come on, come on. Pick up." After several rings, however, his voicemail greeting kicked in. He spoke in impossibly fast French, but her ear could separate the many tones that overlapped each other: professional, serious, a little bit stressed, charismatic, seductive. It was unequivocally Sébastien.

She swallowed. "Um, hi Sébastien. It's me ... Michele. You know, from the plane, and the park. You've been my tour guide for the past couple of days—" *Don't be stupid, Michele. He knows who you are. Get to the point.* "Anyway," she continued, attempting to keep things light, "I'm just wondering where you are? You kind of took off earlier while I was on the phone and I'm, well, I'm a bit worried, actually. I'm not sure what happened but I just want to make sure you're OK, OK?" She unravelled a bit at the edges like a cut piece of fabric; it would only take one tug on the thread to come undone. "Listen, if I did something to upset you, I want to know. I'm sorry if I've been confusing. It has nothing to do with you, I promise. It's this family stuff. I have really, *really* enjoyed our time together, and I'd like to see you again. And if your offer to help me get justice is still on the table, I'm ready to accept ... I like having you on my side." As an afterthought she added, "Call me at the hotel," and hung up.

She plopped onto the bed. "Sébastien, what the heck happened to you?" Or maybe the better question was, what had she done wrong? If there was no emergency, then he had cut and run by choice. And if so, she reasoned, then it must be her fault, though she had no clue where she could have gone wrong. No matter what it was, she could fix it. He could outline his grievances, she would analyze them, and together they would sort out the solutions. If she strategized and put in the effort, she was sure they could work it out, whatever "it" was. The time they'd spent together so far had meant something to both of them, she was convinced of it. There was something real there and it was worth too much to simply walk away now. Michele watched the phone, willing it to ring. "We just need to talk. Come on, Sébastien. I need you." *And just maybe, I love you.*

Unable to sit with the silence, she walked across the room and punched in the code to unlock the safe. She may not have understood Sébastien, and Paris, and what to do when falling for someone, but the diary she could connect with. When it came down to it, it was a historical record after all, and *those* she could comprehend, even if they were confusing or incomplete. She knew where to look for answers. Unlike with emotions, archival processing was so systematic. Who had donated the item? Where had it come from? What were the dimensions and condition? When had it been created, by whom, and why? You just put together as much of the story as you could and then filled in the answers. What you didn't know you left behind. Easy peasy. Often you had to interact with descendants, though Janice was the one at the archives who spoke with them; but mostly, the people you researched and recorded were dead. They told their stories through photographs and documents and whatever details could be added from various resources. The relationship was a quiet one and worked in only one direction. Everything was a lot less complicated that way.

She fingered Clotilde's name on the photocopied inside front cover. *Or at least, it was, until I found you. This was so much simpler when it didn't involve people that I'm actually related to. But now that I know who you are, I have so many questions. What were you like? All I know is what you wrote, and it's not enough. Were you serious, or did you have a great sense of humour? What was my mother like as a child? Would I notice similarities with Henry? How did you cope for all those years after Maurice died? What would you want me to know?*

She blew a bit of fluff from the first page. Ever since finding this book, she had lied, and even crossed a continent and an ocean. It couldn't all be for nothing. There were only a few more days left until she had planned to go home; she would not drop her search at this point. The problem was she now had two different hunts on the go. How could she balance fighting for her family and figuring out the Sébastien situation too?

Diary pages in hand, she picked up her backpack and descended to the ground floor. Maxine was straightening up the lobby, arranging cushions and removing crumpled maps and candy wrappers that had been left on conversation tables or fallen to the floor. On an impulse, Michele detoured to the seating area.

"Uh, *excusez-moi*? I'm really sorry to bother you, but could you help me please?" She changed her mind about asking and took two steps back. *Why does this always feel so weird?* "Or if you're too busy, I could come back later."

"Of course, I am happy to help," Maxine responded. She deposited the wrappers into the trash and smiled broadly. "It would be my pleasure."

"*Merci.* I'm wondering where the nearest hospital would be. Is there one close by?"

"A hospital? There are many in Paris, as well as several *cliniques* within only a few blocks. But I must ask, you are not well? I could phone ahead to the closest one that has the specialty you may need. Not all of them offer the same services." Maxine remained professional but Michele's intuition told her the caring was genuine.

"That is so very kind of you. It's not for me, though." Michele lowered her voice. "I had someone here with me earlier—you probably didn't notice him—"

"I did observe the gentleman with you. It is my job to pay attention to details."

Michele felt like she had found someone on the same wavelength as herself. Maybe Maxine could provide the critical missing information. "You saw him? Was he OK? I was in my room on the phone, he was standing in the doorway, and suddenly he was gone. I've been worried that he was sick or something."

Maxine tilted her head. "I cannot say whether or not he was ill, but he appeared to be very upset when he left."

Well, that doesn't really clear anything up, does it? Michele sighed and took a seat, resting the diary pages on her lap. "Can I ask you something? It might be too personal, so I apologize if it is."

"Yes, pose whatever question you would like. One moment." Maxine took a lap around the lobby, peeking up the stairs and into the back office before sitting down beside her. "If someone comes in, I will have to go," she whispered. "I do not want my boss to catch me here. Now, please go on."

"OK, here it goes. What are French men like in relationships? Or better yet, how would I know if I was in a relationship with one?" Michele stared down at her sneakers.

Maxine responded with a knowing nod. "Ah, *j'comprends. Now* I understand. This man, you met him here in Paris, yes?" Michele blushed but did not speak, so Maxine went on. "I learn a lot about people from working at the hotel. There are, of course, many couples that come here, but there are also single travellers. Some of them are tourists, others are in Paris on business. Occasionally they bring someone back to their room. My job, it requires discretion, so I do not make the judgements, but I will tell you that from my perspective, the difference between what you call in North America the 'hook up' looks very different from a relationship. I can tell right away when the people come down in the morning."

"We most definitely did not *hook up!*" Michele countered.

"Then this is a good first indication. My female friends from England, they tell me that compared to what they are used to at home, they find French men are much more intense. Every date is an occasion, well thought-out and filled with a lot of activity. Typically, the French man will initiate the date and then take care of everything."

"That sounds a lot like the time that Sébastien and I have had together so far." Michele looked up.

"I believe also that relationships move much more quickly here. I think that this is a big cultural difference. The French, we feel the emotions more passionately; we are perhaps more open to them. This intimacy can be strange for people from other countries."

The description certainly seemed to fit. But Michele had to be sure of one more thing. "But, I mean, in Canada, and probably the States, too, we have this idea that all French men have mistresses and flirt with any woman who walks by. Is that true?"

Maxine seemed amused by the question. "Only partially. This is not the case for everyone. In fact, in dating, once you kiss, they consider you to be on an exclusive basis. It becomes a commitment."

In a flash Michele was back on the river cruise, embracing Sébastien as the scenery and the other passengers fell away. She closed her eyes for a moment and opened them to find her confidant studying her. "I, uh, we've had the types of dates you were describing. I just didn't realize they *were* dates. And we did have an incredible kiss on one of those Bateaux Mouches tours earlier today, just before we came here."

"Well, based on what you have told me and from your expression just now, I would say that your relationship is undeniable."

* * *

In a kind of trance, Michele drifted through the empty breakfast room to the courtyard. The diary pages felt heavier than ever, their weight bearing down on her arms. Protected from the sun by the table's red umbrella, the book called her into its photocopied covers. Page by page she used Clotilde's words to travel through the lives of her grandparents and Maurice and, in a way, through her own. Like them, she had made a voyage across the Atlantic. A kind of new start. And like Clotilde, she was a single mom falling in love.

Michele explored the parallels, as if she were comparing two photographs side by side. She read and reread the diary from front to back and soon characters and places merged into a single story: Clotilde and Philippe, Maurice, Edith—herself and Sébastien—back and forth between France and Victoria. She shook her head. Sébastien wasn't connected with her family, or the diary. The only commonality was that he happened to live in the same country her ancestors had come from. He'd been to Canada, but only for a visit so it didn't count. There was the matter of strong mutual attraction, but this was not unique to her grandmother's narrative or her own. English speakers fell for the French all the time; Maxine had seen it first-hand. But the more Michele read, the more confused she became. She rubbed her eyes and stacked the sheets of paper. Maybe it was jet lag, a crash after a buildup of too much adrenaline. Exhaustion and hope were not a sustainable blend. They did strange things to a person.

She mentally retraced her steps, from back when she had first found the diary in the archives right up to that very moment on the Hotel Magellan terrace. Nine days. Nine rotations of the earth for her own world to flip upside down. She got up and skimmed the edge of the table with her fingers as she walked around it. *I keep ending up where I began. I'm not getting anywhere.* There was so much Michele wanted to do, but too much she didn't understand. It was difficult to get anything done with so much uncertainty. She continued to orbit the table.

"Let's see, I haven't looked for the Bouchard's yet so that I can avenge my family, and now I might have lost Sébastien just when we were getting started. That's a big, round zero out of two so far." Michele kept to her path as if it were a meditative labyrinth. Paris was a city for walking. She closed her eyes, using her sense of touch to guide her on a virtual tour. The Arc de Triomphe and Place Charles de Gaulle. Place de la Concorde. The pond at the Luxembourg Gardens. The Ferris wheel and the carousel. But there was something else, and she strained to remember it. There was a pattern there, and if she could make it out, then the idea that was now just out of reach would come to her. The café? No, that wasn't quite right. She pushed a chair in frustration. "Ugh, I'm going around in circles!" *Wait, circles. That's it! I think I know where you might be.*

It wasn't logical, but once the possibility came to her, she couldn't let it go. After all, she and Sébastien were in a relationship—new though it was—and it was worthy of effort. She straightened her chair, picked up the diary pages, and crossed the courtyard, passing back through the dining room before coming to the lobby. As she pushed open the door, she waved in the direction of the front desk. "Thanks again for the advice. It really helped!" Maxine grinned in reply and then turned to greet a guest who had just arrived.

Outside, Michele took the now second-nature route to Boulevard Pereire, back the way she had come from the café. She slapped her forehead. *I was right there! Why didn't I think to look?* This neighbourhood was important to Sébastien; it was his home and he felt a strong connection to this place. Where better to go reset than at its heart? *When something's going on back home, which—let's face it—has been often lately, I end up at Rutledge. Sébastien said that one of his thinking spots was the park inside the Pereire roundabout. Circles. That was the pattern.* He had to be there, she just knew it.

The closer she got, the more she could make out music. As she listened, she realized it was the same she had detected on her initial search along the Promenade and outside the Royale Pereire. The tune was haunting, hanging low in the air like Vancouver Island fog in late October. But it was also elusive, interrupted at irregular intervals by the whine of passing cars. She stood on the far side of the street and inclined her ear. It wasn't a recording; no, someone was definitely playing live. The mysterious musician sent dark and sonorous notes wafting from behind the trees and across the traffic until they encircled her. A shiver ran down her spine despite the afternoon heat. She could hear the instrument clearly now: a violin. She didn't wait for the pedestrian signal; as soon as there was an opening, she tore across the crosswalk and into the park. *Sébastien.* He stood alone at the centre, his back to her. In his hands his great-uncle's violin rocked back and forth like a cradle comforting a child, as if it were holding him up rather than the other way around. Michele inched towards him. She felt like she was intruding on something intimate, even though it was in a public place. Maybe she shouldn't be there. Maybe he didn't want her there.

"Sébastien?" She took another step closer.

He lowered the bow and the violin to his sides and turned to her, languid. His drawn face and defeated manner contrasted alarmingly with the geniality she had come to know. "You found me."

Michele closed the gap between them. "Of course. I would never leave you." She searched his clouded eyes. "Just like you said to me yesterday, remember?"

"Everything was different then. So very different. But now ..." Sébastien shuttered his eyes as tightly as the shops that had closed down for August.

"What are you talking about? Would you just tell me what's going on? Are you sick or hurt? Did something happen to someone in your family? Don't shut me out. Please."

"Hurt? *Je suis brisé.* I am a broken man." He shooed her away with the violin bow when she tried to touch him. "No, it is not my body. I would be able to cope with that, if it were the case. The problem is inside, where it counts the most."

"I don't understand," she uttered. "Was it something I said or did? Tell me, Sébastien. Give me a chance. Let's work it out."

He let out a gloomy sigh and dropped onto a bench. "It was nothing that you or I did. This is something much older than both of us. But the damage is too deep to be undone. It cannot be repaired." He noticed the old handwriting on the diary pages and recoiled. "That was written by your grandmother, was it not?"

"Well, yes, but we don't need to talk about that right now. It has nothing to do with this."

He looked up at the sky with an exasperated, pained expression. "It has everything to do with this!"

"But I don't see—" she began as she brought her face down closer to his.

He grabbed her by the shoulders. "I heard you on the phone. You are seeking out the Bouchard family."

"So what?" She became defensive. "It's the reason I came to Paris. I told you that."

"But you did not share with me their name. I heard it for the first time during your call." Red splotches broke out on his cheeks and his eyes grew watery. "The Bouchard's are my family. They were the ones who caused the great injustice to your grandmother, which also impacted your mother and you. The company that you are going after belongs to my grandfather and will eventually pass to my mother and probably to me."

Michele's blood ran cold. "No. No, that can't be," she stuttered. "There must be some mistake."

"Listen to me. I experienced an incredible shock. I could not think. I knew that I could not stay there. After I left the hotel, I telephoned *Maman* and asked her if she knew anything about my great uncle being involved with a woman in Canada. She tried to— what do you say in English?—'stonewall' me, but I have my ways. She preferred not to discuss this 'ancient history,' but in the end she confirmed everything. It matches all that you have said about your purpose in coming here."

She sat down and her mouth hung open. She searched for something to focus on and found the violin laying mute across Sébastien's legs. "But, but that means—that's Maurice's violin. The same one he played for my grandmother and mother. And you played it for me. Oh my God. This can't be happening."

He ran a hand through his hair. "What are you going to do?"

"I mean, all of this is unbelievable. I had no idea." She clutched the pages to her chest. "But, you have to know how important this is to me. I can't just walk away. This is about my family."

"Michele, this is about mine too. The Bouchard's, and Bouchard Financial, are very much in the public eye. The French media is relentless, and the people *volatil, inconstant.* Quick to change their opinions. The charitable activities of the company have assisted families of reduced means, and the global banking awards will be decided in a matter of months. This is of great importance to my family. What happened to your grandmother—it would give a negative image. If you follow through and the media learns of this, the story, though from decades ago, could damage their—our— reputation.

She leapt up and scowled. "Damage their reputation? The rich, powerful Bouchard family? What about how they treated mine? Does that not count for anything? Besides, I thought you had distanced yourself from them. It's not fair that they can just get away with what they did. You agreed with me. You offered to help. Isn't it about time they paid for their actions?"

Sébastien sprang up to face her. "*Attends*, this is about money for you? I thought that you wanted to speak your mind and to clear the air about the events that took place, not extort them."

"No, it's not like that," she countered. "But the fact of the matter is that my grandmother was destitute when she didn't have to be, and that's a circumstance whose impact has spanned generations. Honestly, I'm struggling too, Sébastien, so yeah, the money would be a life-safer right now. But this is about more than that. This is about meeting my family in the only way I can right now. They cared about me once. I am the only one here who can speak for them. I need this, and so do they."

With his thumb he rubbed the violin like a talisman. "I ... I care for you very much, more than anyone I have met in a long time. But you comprehend how much loyalty means to my family. I have a duty to them."

"Right. Of course you're going to take their side." Michele's eyes stung and she looked away.

"I do not know what to say to make this easier. I must support them—I am sorry."

"Not as much as I am, believe me. I'm sorry I fell for your act. I can't believe I was wined and dined by the heir of a greedy, manipulative man who has no qualms about inflicting hardship on people who can't defend themselves."

"This is not only about you. Please, think of everyone involved. It was so long ago. Do not be selfish," he begged.

Michele volleyed back. "Are you serious right now? You know what, Sébastien? Forget me, and forget whatever I said about you over the past two days. You are just like them. I guess we'll each do what we have to do."

CHAPTER 9

In the midst of the chaos, I have become a mother. My life story is now forever linked with that of my daughter, and with those of her future children. I feel a continuity in seeing myself and Philippe in her. (She has his distinctive grey eyes. I would recognize them anywhere). Philippe, Edith and I are a family, and no matter what happens during this war and beyond, nothing can ever erase that link. The bond of blood endures, and I am certain that the immense love that I feel at this moment will carry on past my lifetime to touch my descendants as if I were there with them.

I am told that the name Edith means "riches." She certainly is a jewel, a gift in this time of darkness. And I shall fight for her with all the love that is her birthright, and provide her with the prosperity that is her namesake. If war were to reach these shores and touch us, I would give everything I had to keep her safe. In the end, our family is all that we have.

* * *

Friday, August 21, 2009

After a fitful night of tossing and turning, made more uncomfortable by the hard mattress, at 6:00 a.m. Michele gave up on sleep. Sweat-drenched, she dragged herself to the bathroom and ran a lukewarm shower. Her bloodshot and puffy eyes followed her through the mirror and dared her to let yesterday's events swallow her again like a second wave. They knew it was not the mattress that had kept her awake for most of the night. She didn't cave in. Instead, she let the spray hit her body like pellets, each strike giving her the ammunition she needed for the battle ahead. She used the miniature bar of soap to saturate a washcloth with foam and then scrubbed her skin raw, attacking the places Sébastien had touched her: her shoulders, her hands, her lips. She would begin the day with a clean slate.

Despite her new determination, however, she couldn't keep the memories at bay. They had already been carefully affixed and captioned, sepia images in an album that would never be filled. The first pages held photographs of riding the Vespa around Paris, enjoying an authentic French picnic, dancing at Pigalle. Even simple things like watching *High Fidelity* and sitting in the park at the Promenade had been included. Now she had to tear them all out and throw them away. There was nothing there that merited permanent retention in her personal archives.

She gave herself a final, long rinse and came out of the shower reinvigorated. With the diversions now out of the picture, she could give all her focus to the task at hand. It was time to finally get answers. "So, what do you wear when your plan for the day is to seek out truth and justice?" she wondered aloud as she rummaged through her suitcase. She hadn't packed any kind of power outfit for the occasion—not that she owned one—so she settled on a simple floral dress and hoped it looked, if not professional, at least somewhat polished. After securing her hair in a small, messy bun at the nape of her neck, she left her room and padded down the hall, cognizant that most guests were probably still in bed. It was not until she had made it down the stairs that she switched from her light steps and strode to the front desk. Maxine stopped typing and greeted her in her usual, sunny manner.

"*Bonjour!* Good morning! Were you successful in locating your *friend?*" She emphasized the last word with a knowing look. "I hope that you found him and were able to spend an enjoyable evening together."

Michele's face hardened but she kept her composure. "Actually, we have parted ways. No, it's fine," she added before Maxine could comment. "I have important business to attend to today as part of my project. Would you kindly look up the phone number and address of a company for me?"

"Oh, I see. My apologies. Yes, of course." Maxine appeared rattled as she placed her fingers along the keyboard. "What is the name, *Mademoiselle?*"

"It's Bouchard Financial. Have you heard of it?"

Maxine kept her eyes on the screen as she tapped the keys. "Yes, it has existed for a long time. It is a very large and well known company in France, particularly here in Paris where the headquarters are located." She transcribed text from the screen onto the blank edge of a map and marked locations before handing it to Michele. "Here is their contact information. Their offices should be open in about one hour from now."

"Thank you." Michele opened her mouth to say something more but changed her mind. She had gotten what she'd come for, so there was no need for any frivolous chit chat, even if she did have an hour to kill.

In her room, she spent the next sixty-two minutes pacing, tidying her things, making the bed—twice—and arranging her toiletries by size, type, and colour. When the bedside clock turned over to 8:00 a.m., she picked up the phone and made the call. A disinterested female answered on the third ring.

"*Compagnie Financière Bouchard, bonjour.*"

"Yes, *bonjour. Parlez-vous anglais?* Do you happen to speak English?"

The receptionist sighed and responded, "How may I assist you?"

"I need to speak with Mr. Bouchard."

"*Monsieur Bouchard?* The president of the company?"

"Yes, that's the one."

"He is a very busy man and does not accept calls from the public. I could put you through to one of our agents, or to a manager, if the question is more involved. They will be able to help you with your financial matter."

"I'm sorry, I guess I'm not expressing myself very well. This 'financial matter' directly involves Mr. Bouchard. It's something he needs to handle personally." Michele would not get anywhere if she didn't keep pushing.

"*Madame*, it is not possible. The people with whom he speaks, they already know how to reach him."

"I see. Well, perhaps you might pass a message on to him, then. Now, be sure to write this down; I don't want anything left out. I need to talk to Mr. Bouchard about his late brother's fiancée from Canada and how she was treated by Bouchard Financial following his death. I am the granddaughter of that woman. She was *Clotilde Joseph*," Michele drew out the name. "I'm sure Mr. Bouchard will understand what I'm referring to. Now—and here's the most important part—if I don't hear back within the next two hours about a meeting today, I will have no choice but to go public with the story. It would be a shame if something were to be published online and sent out to various media outlets, especially given the company's recent award nomination. Not a good look for a business that supposedly cares about downtrodden families. Oh, and my name is Michele Norman. You can reach me at the Hotel Magellan. Did you get all of that?"

The silence on the other end confirmed she'd gotten her point across. The terse receptionist regained her voice. "I will see what I can do," she replied and hung up.

At that point there was nothing to do but wait. "I guess I might as well get some breakfast," Michele said before heading downstairs. Bypassing the croissants and figs, she gravitated towards the toaster and inserted a slice of bread into it. There was something to be said for simple. She'd tried French food—been there, done that—but now she craved the basics. An everything bagel would have to be on the menu when she got back to Victoria. She carried her plate and her glass of orange juice to the courtyard and chose an empty table. Once again the air sat hot and humid above her, but the sky begged to tear itself apart and release the pressure with a refreshing rain. *If only it would come. I could go for a heavy storm, just like the ones at home.* She longed for steady showers, no matter how cold, and the ocean's salty bite. In vain she watched for drops to fall; the gathering clouds were not yet ready to let go.

A few nibbles into her plain toast, she abandoned her meal and slid the plate to the far side of the table. What if the Bouchard's refused to speak with her? She had talked a big game on the phone, but if it came down to it she wasn't sure she would have the nerve to go through with her threat. Her words had belonged to a stranger. She had not recognized that assertive, demanding person at all, as if her true self had been temporarily taken over by a far mightier force. It wasn't her.

She watched a sparrow hop around her feet hunting for crumbs. The thought of airing the Bouchard dirty laundry gave her pause, but the reality of landing a meeting with them was downright terrifying. It was one thing to imagine it, but quite another to be there in person. What would she say? There was no script for this sort of situation. It wasn't every day you found your long-lost family—and then had to go head to head against a corporate powerhouse to avenge them. Although the opportunity to interrogate the Bouchard's had always been the end goal, she had no plan. Where would she even begin if she managed to get into that room?

Well, it was all moot if they didn't respond. Michele left the courtyard, proceeded through the dining area, and mounted the stairs to her floor. Inside her room, a flashing red light on the phone flagged her like a flare. Her insides tumbled, organs crashing into one another as a cold blast crested up her body. No matter what happened, she was going to hit the shore; the question was whether or not she would break up on the beach like so many abandoned sailboats and dinghies at Cadboro Bay. She picked up the phone to retrieve the message. Her words more clipped than earlier, the same receptionist delivered a curt statement. "*Madame* Norman, I have been instructed to ask that you be at the Bouchard offices in one hour. It is currently 8:30. Please check in with the security desk and then continue to room 1022 on the tenth floor. Take note that this offer is extended as a courtesy and is of a limited duration. Do not be late."

Michele's heart hammered against her chest. *It's really happening.* She hung up and opened the map Maxine had provided. Following the pen lines from the *X* indicating the hotel to the circled area labelled "Bouchard," she could see the company was located at the centre of La Défense, the major business district. "OK, so it looks like it's just a straight shot northwest from the Arc de Triomphe. That seems easy enough," she said as she studied the map more closely. "And there's an arch there as well? It's really close to Bouchard Financial, so that should be a good landmark to watch for. Now, how to get there, and within the next hour." Resisting a sudden urge to pull the reproduction diary out of the safe, she instead grabbed a Métro map from the top of the desk. She read the time on the clock and quickened her pace. "Check that, make it 45 minutes ..."

* * *

West-bound, the Métro Line 1 terminated at La Défense-Grande Arche. Michele rode the escalator to the surface and blinked as her eyes adjusted. After travelling through the subterranean tunnels that traversed the city, she found the natural light all the brighter in contrast; at least, at first. When the escalator deposited her at ground level, she did a double take. The wide plaza walled in by modern buildings could have been in Vancouver—rigid skyscrapers of steel and glass had replaced the curves and warmth that gave Paris its allure. Unlike the captivating Montmartre or Place de la Concorde, La Défense loomed brash and unapologetic, dominating everything and everyone in its shadow—the City of Light's darker timeline. Even the Grande Arche, a severe cube installed directly above the Métro station, seemed like a sinister version of the Arc de Triomphe. An evil twin.

She consulted the map and oriented herself. Heeding the directions she'd put together from Maxine's information, she crossed the plaza and turned left after the shopping centre, deciding at the last minute to take a surprise passageway rather than going all the way around. *If I'm right, this should, in theory, come out right across from the offices.* She kept her head down as she exited from the other side of the pedestrian access and barrelled down the wide steps. She lifted her gaze. Ahead and to her left, a mirrored black tower looked down upon the structures around it. Emblazoned in green and gold at the top corner some forty floors above the street was simply the name "Bouchard" as if no further explanation were needed.

"Right. Of *course* that's the one I have to go to." She threw her arms open in surrender. "It couldn't be any of these other, boring buildings. It had to be the one that looks like a supervillain headquarters." Henry would have said it was LexCorp, where Lex Luther was plotting his next move against Superman. It was fitting, but it didn't make her any less apprehensive. *Well, 'fake it 'till you make it'? Is that the right phrase in this situation?* Michele imagined putting on a superhero mask. She covered her face with an artificial expression of confidence and stomped the rest of the way to the high-rise. At the entrance, her eyes burned as she ran them all the way up the outside of the building; the obsidian walls magnified and reflected the sun's fierce rays back at her like a weapon designed to make her weaker. *No, don't let them take you down.* She scrunched her face and tensed all her muscles before letting everything go. "OK, you've got this."

The door opened and a bike courier whizzed by, bumping her shoulder.

"Oh, excuse me," she replied automatically, even though she wasn't at fault. When he didn't reciprocate, she grabbed the door before it closed and stood in the entryway, staring after him. Her regular Canadian politeness was not going to work today, she realized. To succeed, she would have to call on that alternate version of herself that had come out on the phone. She carried that thought with her to the security desk, where a beefy middle-aged man in uniform assessed her with suspicion.

"*Bonjour.*" He looked her over and continued in English. "Please state your business here," he demanded. Apparently her Canadian-ness was more obvious than she realized.

"I have an appointment with Mr. Bouchard." She pointed at his clipboard. "Right here. Michele Norman." There wasn't time to read the note beside her name, but she had a pretty good idea what it said.

"*Attendez.*" The guard pressed a button on his lapel radio and turned his back to her, speaking in a low voice. A moment later he came out from behind the desk and chaperoned her to an elevator. "They are expecting you in conference room 1022. Please go there directly. Do not make any detours," he ordered. "We would not want you to get lost, *Mademoiselle.*"

"Wait, *they?*" she asked, as the guard reached in to select the floor. The doors sealed shut, leaving her to wonder on the way up if she'd heard him correctly.

Minutes later Michele found herself standing outside 1022. Everything rode on what happened on the other side of that door. She would learn whether or not her questionable choices of late had been worth it. Inside, the room was cavernous—much larger than she'd expected. Floor to ceiling windows, with no trace of their black exterior, made up the far wall. The only furniture was a massive, rectangular boardroom table with padded chairs spaced evenly along both lengths. In the row opposite her, the man at the centre of the Bouchard website photo now appeared in the same position, this time presiding from a large, leather Chairman's seat. His age-spotted and veined hands drummed the tabletop as if he were biding his time. A striking woman had taken the place to his right. While she was younger than Mr. Bouchard and dressed head to toe in haute couture, her resemblance to him was too obvious to ignore. Without a doubt Michele was looking at the Bouchard patriarch and his daughter, first and second in command. To his left, silent and still as a statue from the Luxembourg Gardens, sat another member of the family: Sébastien.

She searched his vacant eyes. He was a bust, unmoving, put out on display to what—rattle her? Or maybe this had been his true self all along, and she was observing it for the first time. *Let's face it, he probably warned them yesterday that I was coming.* After all, even though he didn't carry the Bouchard name on paper, he was one of them. It would have been easy for her to go back and scrutinize the days they had spent together, combing every moment for some indication of his identity—but what did it matter now? That ship had sailed. Like their river boat cruise down the Seine, it was over. Sooner or later, the kiss and everything that had led up to it would mean nothing. She would feel nothing. Despite this conviction, she tried to attract his attention with her eyes, willing him to regard her the way he had before, just one last time. Sébastien, however, remained lifeless.

Alone on her side of the table, Michele sat down across from his grandfather. Without any preamble Mr. Bouchard called the meeting to order. "*Mademoiselle* Norman, I understand that you have been conducting some research on my family's history and have some questions to pose. Of course, all of that is from the distant past. I cannot see what importance it could possibly have now." He smiled like the Cheshire Cat. "But we have found some time in our very busy schedules to clarify any—misunderstandings. My daughter, Berdine," he nodded, then added suggestively, "and I believe that you have already met my grandson, Sébastien."

"Uh, yes. Um, I mean, no. I mean, thank you for agreeing to see me," Michele replied, stumbling over her words before remembering the aggressive approach she'd planned. *Don't let them throw you off. Just stick to the facts.* "Well, I'll get right to it, then. I'm from Victoria, British Columbia, Canada. I've recently learned that my grandparents were from France. They were married in Victoria, but my grandfather came back here as a pilot in WWII. Sadly, he was killed in action. My grandmother, Clotilde Joseph, was left on her own with my mother, Edith, who was just a young child at the time. However, Clotilde met Maurice Bouchard and they fell in love." She snuck a split-second glance at Sébastien, but his head was down, hands clasped on top of the table. "And, um, they had decided to spend the rest of their lives together. But before they could marry, Maurice died. Now, according to my grandmother, he had wanted his fiancée and stepchild to always be looked after. I'm here today because you, Mr. Bouchard, did not honour your brother's wishes. Because of that, my family was left to struggle for years, while you became richer and built your empire."

Berdine responded first. Looking Michele up and down, she spread her lips in a slow sneer. "Such a charming story," she purred. "Almost as charming as your quaint fashion choice. But why are you *really* here? What do you want, *hein*?"

"Oh!" Michele found herself at a loss for words. She turned to Sébastien; he had raised a hand to his forehead, obscuring his eyes and keeping any reaction hidden. How could he just sit there and not say anything?

"My daughter's poor manners notwithstanding," Mr. Bouchard intervened, "we must ask you: what are you hoping to accomplish by coming to us now?"

"I ... I want justice. I want what my grandmother and mother should have had, what was rightfully theirs. I want Maurice's estate."

"I see. I thought that might be the case," he said. "*Mais*, the problem for you is that you have no legal claim to anything. Tell me, how exactly is it that you came to know about my brother's supposed ill-advised romance and his alleged *wishes*? Surely you have brought some official documents?" Mr. Bouchard's loaded shrug hung in the air; it was just like Sébastien's. Michele felt sick.

"My grandmother told me everything herself—in her diary. And it fits with what I found through my research."

"Well, my dear, a diary is certainly a keepsake of sentimental value—personally I have never kept one myself because there are many things that I would not want captured in writing—but they have no bearing on judicial proceedings, particularly without any supporting documentation. *De plus*, the events that you are relating, if they are indeed true, occurred over sixty years ago. Our company has proven its commitment to helping the less fortunate, and our reputation will hold. You, on the other hand, will be perceived as opportunistic should you pursue this ridiculous claim. Then there is the most salient point: Maurice was never married. This reality cannot be disputed. So you see, no court would decide in your favour should you continue on this misguided effort. You may ask any expert."

"And," Berdine chimed in, "this is assuming that you could afford the representation, which undoubtedly you cannot." She inspected her manicured nails and ran them through her sleek hair.

Michele's facts and logic drained away into the plush carpet before she even realized they were gone. She stood and shook a finger at the senior Bouchard. "OK, let's say I don't have any legal standing here. But what about your moral and ethical obligation, huh? Your brother truly *loved* my grandmother. They were meant to be together, and that was taken away from them by circumstances outside their control. Their love was real! You could honour your brother's memory by honouring that," she pleaded.

"My brother was a fool!" Mr. Bouchard shot up out of his seat and banged the table with his fists. Regaining his composure, he resumed the chair. "He was always too *émotif*. It kept him from achieving his full potential and eventually took him away from the company that we had created together. We had—different ideas about the future direction for our business. If we had followed his idealism, we would never have prospered, especially during the war. Luckily when he went to Canada, he left the decision-making to me. It has paid off. I had hoped that he would one day see reason and return, but he put his energies into matters of the heart and then he was gone, *comme ça*. If only he had chosen the more sensible path." He leaned back and sighed.

"That's it? That's your story?" Michele said, choking on her words. "Did you even bother to learn *anything* about my grandmother?"

"*Mademoiselle* Norman, I preferred to know as little as possible about Maurice's Canadian amusements. My duty was, and still is, to grow and protect the family legacy. I am sure that you can understand that. Now, if there are no more questions ..."

An invisible strap tightened around her chest, constricting her breathing. "Just one. I realize this was much later, but do you have any knowledge at all of what became of Clotilde's daughter? Do you know what happened to her, after she—she disappeared in the early 1980s. I want to find her."

"I do not, nor is it any of my concern. After my brother's death, we moved on. You would be wise to do the same. Please see yourself out."

Michele unceremoniously wiped a fat tear with the back of her arm and ran out of the room.

* * *

The doors parted and she stepped out of the subway car. She remembered staggering from the conference room and making her way outside but had no recollection of the trip to Pereire. There was no way she could even have thought to find three things. When she came up from the Métro station to the roundabout, drops landed on her face and roused her. The sky had turned charcoal. Completely saturated, the clouds threw down their precipitation more and more ferociously as she slogged back along the boulevard. It didn't take long for the rain to come down in full force. As her flats squished under her chilled feet, she debated slinking back underground to hide. Things had not gone the way they were supposed to, and she did not know where to go from there. The Bouchard's had been even worse than Sébastien had let on, and she would have given anything to have never met any of them—or, to mercifully wipe her memory clean of it all. The worst part was they were right about everything. She shouldn't have come. Maybe it would have been better if she'd never found the diary in the first place.

She arrived outside the hotel, drenched. Her bun had come apart, the elastic lost somewhere along the way, and her sopping hair acted as a conduit, sending rain down her neck and under her dress. The deluge raged on, but she stayed on the sidewalk and let the water consume the uncontrollable sobs that had broken out.

"What am I doing here?" Michele screamed into the empty street. There was nothing left for her in Paris anymore. What had she been thinking? Everything she had ever needed had been in Victoria all along, yet she'd never appreciated it. Her body heaved with remorse. How many ways had she failed her son? In his innocence he accepted her as she was, but she left him over and over again— just like her father had done to her—for what? Pure selfishness. She had put her own needs above Henry's, when she should have known better than anyone the hurt of abandonment.

What about Mrs. Eliades? *How could I not see that I was taking advantage of her while pushing her away?* She was not her grandmother or mother, but she was family just like Amanda and John and Barbara. Michele had tried to do everything on her own, when she should have acknowledged she needed help and that there were people who wanted to be part of her life. It had been right in front of her the whole time, but she'd been too blind to see it. *That* was what she had to make right, not this sixty-year-old fight and definitely not her relationship with Sébastien, no matter how destined a couple they had seemed. It was time to let her family—past and present—in. It was time to go home.

Soaked, she blew into the lobby, leaving a spray of water in her wake as an astonished Maxine looked on. Michele didn't stop. When she got into her room, she stripped off her clothes and threw on clean shorts and a T-shirt before collapsing on the bed. In the background the phone tolled, sounding farther away until the ringing ceased altogether. Tears ran freely down her cheeks and mirrored the rain streaming against the window. On the glass, a montage of her life played in a loop, the distorted pictures edited together with no regard for chronology: giving birth to Henry—alone—at Victoria General Hospital; delighting in an afternoon of horse riding lessons—a gift from John and Barbara—on her seventh birthday; drinking wine with Sébastien during the flight to Paris; pulling an all-nighter with Amanda to cram for their biology final. Even as Michele's eyes closed, the images came faster and more focused. She watched Sébastien calming her on the Ferris wheel; Mrs. Eliades dancing in the kitchen, holding a framed photo of Dimitri; a beautiful woman smiling from above, wiping her hands on a blue apron.

Michele reached out to her with a yearning she'd never let herself feel before, and willed herself to draw the woman close enough to see her face. In the past, Michele had always shut down the upsetting visions before the woman could get near. Now, her grey eyes sparkled, full of life and laughter and love. She swayed and twirled, and parted her lips to speak but was mute.

"Please!" Michele cried. "I need you. I'm ready now. Please let me remember you." The woman nodded warmly and tried again. Familiar lyrics drifted to Michele's ears, and this time they did not set off a panic—but rather told a story—her story. "Mom? Mom, it's you! I miss you so much. And Grandma too. I found out she passed away a long time ago. You didn't have to go. We would have found a way to survive. I wish we could go back and be together again, like we once were. There's so much I want to tell you. You have a grandson now! You would *love* Henry, and I'm sure he would be crazy about you too. Did you know he has your eyes? I'd always wondered where they came from. If you were with us, you could sing to him, too, just like you did to me all the time ... Please, I have to find you." Michele wept and Edith stroked her hair, rocking her daughter with the faint echoes of the song they shared from another time and place.

* * *

Michele woke up to the sound of her name. "What?" She groaned and the events of that day came flooding back. She sat up, swung her legs over the edge of the bed, and saw that two hours had passed; it was mid-afternoon. Bleary-eyed, she went to the window. At some point the rain had stopped and the late-day sun spilled between the buildings on Rue Jean-Baptiste Dumas, erasing almost all signs of the storm. A smattering of puddles decorated the road like precious stones and caught the light from the now vivid sky. By the looks of it, Paris had come through the bout of nasty weather unscathed. But, wondered Michele, had she? It hadn't been real, her mom being there—how could it be? But Michele had seen and heard her. Whether or not it had been a dream was inconsequential. She may have thought she'd found her mom in the diary, but the discovery hadn't been complete until Michele had finally *felt* her with all the genuine and complicated emotions that had been stored for so many years but never accessed. After all her refusal and avoidance, she had her mom back, in a matter of speaking, until Michele could track her down and see her in person. It was the first meaningful step in connecting with her family; the inquiry going forward wasn't going to be only about facts, but feelings too.

Family. *Her* family. The words made her tingle, and she welcomed them. She had a lot of catching up to do at home. Maybe when she got back, she could take Henry to Rutledge Park. She'd been there so often by herself, but now they would go together, after school come September, and it would be about him. Yes, she would lift him up onto the pink elephant and hang on to every word of the adventures that he imagined on Rutley while she made sure he didn't slip off. They could play superheroes at home if it was too wet to go out. Oh! Maybe they could even convince Mrs. Eliades to join in too. Michele snorted. It would be quite the sight. But thinking about school and Mrs. Eliades also brought her financial problems back to the forefront. She was no closer to a solution.

"No more excuses," Michele resolved as she gathered her belongings. "I don't care if I need to find a second job. I'll even leave the archives if I have to, though I love the work. If I need to ask Amanda or my adoptive parents for help, then so be it. We're family. We can work it out and even come up with a fair payback arrangement we all agree on." She opened her suitcase and tossed her things inside. "It's called being an adult, Michele, and it's time to do that. Enough with hanging on to some ridiculous idea about living my lost youth. It's done."

With the suitcase open, she went to the safe, unlocked it, and took out the pages. They'd told her everything they could and now she could let the diary go. She could let it all go. At its core, the story was a moving account from the wartime years in Victoria, and it should be available to everyone. When she returned to the archives she would sit down with Janice and come clean about everything. Tell her everything she'd found out, so it could be shared. Then, regardless of whether or not Janice fired her for her deception, Michele would put things right, for the future. A gift form signed by a descendant, along with all the background information and provenance she could provide, would make the donation official.

As she bundled up the pages and secured them in her backpack, she spied a piece of paper on the carpet near the door. *I must have dropped something while I was packing.* She walked over and crouched down to have a look. "That's weird." It was a plain white paper napkin, but she had never brought one back with her from breakfast; in fact, other than the Royale Pereire she hadn't eaten in restaurants at all. She snatched it from the ground, preparing to crumple it up and lobby it into the trash can. As she stood up, however, she noticed a pop of colour and some writing on the other side. "What's this?" A red logo on the top corner identified the origin of the napkin. It had come from the café. *Sébastien's* café. In the middle was a note in ball point pen: the last line of the song "Michelle" followed by the words "Please meet me.—Séb."

CHAPTER 10

I am not at all surprised that Philippe has joined the fight, only that it has taken him this long to do so. My first impression of him two years ago was not mistaken; in fact, it has only been magnified with time. He is the strongest person that I have ever known, courageous and daring in action, but also introspective and unaware of his own abilities. My concern is that in the air, his tendency to impulsiveness will override the good judgment that too often comes in second place.

There was never any question of his joining the air force. Philippe was born to fly. In open, endless spaces he finds a freedom where I would see emptiness. Just as I believe I am beginning to truly understand him, he leaves; first for training in Vancouver, and then to Europe. The girl in me longs to keep him for myself, hidden and safe like a treasure. In the end, however, doing what is right must prevail over satisfying the heart. The only way forward is acceptance.

* * *

Friday, August 21, 2009

"Are you kidding me? Of all the nerve ..." Michele balled up the napkin and threw it in the garbage. How dare he try to contact her now. Did he really think he could just summon her like that? That she would come running? No. She would not give him the opportunity to twist the knife deeper. There'd been enough damage already.

She busied herself inspecting the room to make sure she had everything, slowing down each time she walked near the mesh bin.

By her third pass, the napkin had unfurled itself, and the red, which evoked the Royale Pereire's awning, implored her to take notice.

"Ugh, this is ridiculous," she exclaimed, closing in on the can. "What did Mr. Bouchard advise me to do? Move on. Well, Sébastien, how about I start with you. Let's end this once and for all." She fished the napkin out and stretched it between her hands, ready to tear it into as many tiny pieces as possible. "Goodbye, Sébastien." She closed her eyes and saw him as he had been at the Bouchard Financial offices: stone-faced and distant. If she destroyed his note, then that frigid version would be the last picture she ever had of him. Maybe she should hear him out. After all, he had made the effort to contact her. She wouldn't know if what he had to say was important unless she met with him one last time.

On the other hand, she didn't want to be pulled back in. The mere fact that he was waiting at the café made her tingle deep in her core, despite her most reasoned logic telling her she was finished with him. If she walked into that café, one of two things could happen: he would rake her over the coals to finish the job his grandfather and mother had started in the conference room, or she would forget her indignation and run into his arms. Both outcomes were bad. But if she didn't go, she would never get closure. Brows furrowed, she smoothed out the napkin against the wall. Why couldn't someone just tell her what to do?

What she needed was a neutral third party. No, wait, that wasn't quite accurate, she thought. What she *actually* needed was someone to really listen and give her honest advice. It was the wee hours of the morning in British Columbia so Amanda and the kids would be in bed, not to mention John and Barbara and Mrs. Eliades. Michele tapped her lips as she deliberated. *You know, it's high time I finally got myself another friend. I think I'm long overdue.* She rushed downstairs with the napkin in hand, hoping she wasn't too late.

When she arrived at the front desk, however, a male clerk was logging into the computer and organizing documents for the second shift. "No!" she blurted, causing him to give her a quizzical look. "I mean, sorry. *Je m'excuse.*" She dropped into one of the lobby chairs. *I can't believe I just missed her! Can I please have one thing go my way? Is that too much to ask?* As if answering her plea, the door behind the front desk opened and Maxine came out carrying an oversized handbag; her work suit had been swapped out for fashionable street clothes. She waved to her colleague and took her leave, crossing the floor and walking towards the exit.

This is my chance! Michele jumped up and called out, "Maxine! Hey! Can I talk to you for a minute?" Sensing hesitation, she begged. "Please?"

Maxine inched closer. "I have just finished work for the day, but Damien would be pleased to assist you, *Mademoiselle.*"

"Please, call me Michele. And this isn't a hotel issue, it's personal."

"I do not know about—"

"Listen, I understand if you want to distance yourself from me after how I behaved. I'm sorry about earlier. I was snippy with you, and I feel really bad about it. You've been so nice to me during my stay, and beyond the whole employee-guest relationship, I thought we were maybe becoming friends. And honestly, I could use a friend right now."

Maxine yielded and Michele caught the hint of a smile. "I accept your apology. From our conversations and from my own observations, I believe that your visit to Paris has been somewhat complicated."

"That's an understatement! And on top of it all, I'm not good at the making friends thing—as you can see," she said, reddening. "But I'm working on that."

"Well, Michele, I generally make a point of not fraternizing with guests—it is an unofficial hotel policy. But as you may recall, I have already broken this rule in your case. I must admit, I am glad for the opportunity to do so again. Now, come with me. We will go to the terrace."

"But what about your boss? I don't want you to get in trouble."

Unruffled, Maxine led her outside. "He is not here. Besides this, we will not be drawing attention to ourselves since I am no longer in uniform. *En outre*," she said, as they reached the courtyard, "I am on my own time. Therefore, there is no problem."

The afternoon had dispersed the hotel's residents throughout the city to explore the sights. It was true that Michele and Maxine would not bother anyone because they had the entire space to themselves. Primed for conversation, they opted for the closest table. Michele had barely sat down when she launched into her story, beginning with the most recent development.

"So, here's where I'm at. My friend—his name is Sébastien—slipped this note under my door sometime this afternoon," she began, displaying the wrinkled napkin for Maxine to see. "And I know that you know that he's more than a friend; you said yourself that you pay attention to details. Anyway, he *was* more than a friend. Or at least, I thought he was. The thing is, there's a major obstacle between us now. Like, I'm talking a giant wall. There's no way around it. I had accepted we were done, but then this stupid napkin appeared and confused everything."

Maxine raised one eyebrow and half-closed the other eye. "In my experience, very few challenges in life are completely without any solution. There are usually some options to improve the situation."

"Not this time. Do you remember that 'project' I'm supposed to be doing here?"

"I do not know much about it, other than it involved the Bouchard company, I believe."

"Yes. It's all very convoluted, but I came to Paris to confront the Bouchard family about something they did to my grandmother and mother a long time ago—I just found out about it recently myself. But then I met Sébastien, and it was a very—pleasant, though unrelated, addition to this trip—or so I thought. It turns out our family histories intersect, and not in a good way. He's a Bouchard!" Michele filled in the rest of the details, laying out the entire drama in reverse order and ending with the diary.

"But, that is incredible!" Maxine declared. "It is like something from a film! And now he would like to see you. Hmm, I can better understand the difficulty that you are facing. What are you doing to do?"

"I don't know! That's why I came to you." Michele made a nest of her hair as she spoke. "Do I go to the café, or do I just cut my losses and get out of here? I have a lot waiting for me back home. Maybe I should just leave it alone and head to the airport?"

"As your friend, I am going to ask you to ask yourself a question: what is it that is really holding you back from meeting with him? You must tell the truth, at least to yourself."

Michele mulled it over. If her new acceptance of friendship was going to stand a chance, she had to start being honest with people. Why *was* she so torn about meeting Sébastien? She debated which was the scarier prospect: having him yell at her, or hearing him say that in spite of everything he felt the same butterflies about her that she still had for him. If she walked into the Royale Pereire and the reality turned out to be the latter, what did that even mean? They couldn't erase the past, no matter how much they wanted to. She sighed.

"The truth is, I was falling in love with him. I've never been in love before, and honestly, I haven't looked for it. This came out of nowhere and it was sweet and perfect and beautiful and all the things I never thought I could feel—I never *let* myself feel."

"Then perhaps you should trust in this feeling?" Maxine suggested.

"But I did, and look where it got me! I'm not sure it was worth it." Michele leaned back in her chair and stretched her legs out, pointing and flexing her toes. "Do you know that we kissed? I think I told you he took me on one of those Bateaux Mouches tours on the river yesterday. And it didn't feel like he was, you know, setting himself up to make a move or anything. It just happened. This is going to sound corny, but it was like time stopped for a second. Do you know what I mean?"

Maxine grinned; evidence, Michele thought, of first-hand knowledge. "Absolutely! That is what true love is supposed to feel like. Not everyone is fortunate enough to experience it during their lifetime. And there is no better place to find it than here. You *do* know that Paris is called the City of Love, yes?"

"Well, of course I do. But I just don't think it can work for me and Sébastien. There are too many external factors involved." Michele folded her legs under her seat and leaned forward again. She fidgeted until Maxine took hold of her forearms.

"You asked for my advice, and I am ready to give it to you. Go and talk with him. Maybe it goes well and maybe it does not; this you cannot know in advance. But if nothing else, it will bring this chapter to a definite close for you one way or the other. Otherwise you will doubtless be left to wonder what would have happened."

"I don't know. I guess you have a point."

"Trust me, it will be liberating. Now you must leave! I believe that someone is waiting for you."

"Alright, alright, I'm going. I just hope you're right about this." Michele got up and started for the door, turning back before she stepped inside. "And thank you. Your support means a lot."

"That is what friends are for."

* * *

The distance from the Hotel Magellan to the Royale Pereire felt at once longer than ever and somehow not long enough. On route, Michele turned the same thought over and over in her mind. She had used the L-word. The admission left her dumbfounded as she closed the gap between her and her destination. Loving Sébastien, however, was not on the table—even if that table was of the delightful bistro variety. He had taken his family's side. He'd let them attack her. There was no coming back from that—was there? Yet she couldn't help but wonder if by some miracle he had loved her too. Would there be some faint trace of it, like pale ink on an old letter, that she would be able to make out when she saw him?

Soon the red café awning beckoned her through the boulevard trees. She turned right at the roundabout and tempered her speed. There could be any number of reasons for Sébastien wanting to see her, and the same number of ways things could play out. The answer waited amongst the sidewalk tables coming into view. She crossed the last street and continued to the only table that mattered. At his regular spot, hair disheveled and cheeks drawn, Sébastien stood up to meet her.

"I did not know if you would come." His voice was hoarse.

Michele searched his face and detected an emotion she couldn't identify. Relief? Anticipation? Hope? It did not seem to be disgust or hate, and for that small gift she was grateful. "Well, neither did I. I wasn't going to, to be honest, but then a friend convinced me I should."

"Then I am forever indebted to them. Please, sit."

She did, but cringed at his use of a financial term; she didn't need any reminders related to owing money. "Fine, but I'm really not sure what's left to say. Not that you said anything in that boardroom this morning. I guess your grandfather and mother covered everything, huh?"

He locked eyes with her. "I was horrified by their behaviour. Please understand that their only objective is to protect our company."

"Our?" She stiffened. "I thought you weren't even involved. That you wanted to keep your distance from their craziness and start your own law firm."

"Yes, that was always my goal. You know how important that was to me. And for the record, I strongly disagree with my family's methods. This situation has been extremely difficult, especially considering the feelings that I have developed for you during our time together." His expression was pained. "*Mais ça ne fait rien maintenant.* It does not matter now."

"Doesn't matter? Are you saying that whatever it was that we had is worth nothing? You left me a note just so you could tell me this to my face? Well, you shouldn't have bothered." She pushed her chair back to go but Sébastien grabbed her hand and pulled her close.

"Michele. *Attends.* You misunderstand me. Our 'unexpected' relationship," he said with meaning, "it was *everything.*"

In his doleful eyes she recognized the truth. But while he'd answered one question, he had left her with many more. "Then I'm really confused," she confessed.

"*Ecoute-moi.* I would love nothing more than to be your French tour guide forever. But do you recall the history I told you at Place de La Concorde of the obelisks? They were separated by circumstances beyond their control, destined to spend the rest of their days on different continents. *Ceci, c'est nous.* It is us."

"I get it. With what happened between our families, we could never work." She picked at her ragged fingernails. "Well, thanks for clearing that up. I should go."

"That is not the reason why we must be apart—let me explain. You came to Paris to 'make things right,' as you had told me, and my family, they prevented you from doing this. But I found a way for you to at last have the justice that you deserve."

"What are you talking about?"

"I was disgusted for not speaking up when my grandfather and mother were treating you so terribly. My lack of action was shameful. But after you left the conference room, I was able to redeem myself."

"What? What did you do?"

For a split-second he metamorphosed back to his old, confident self, but a layer of sadness still came through the veneer. "I did what I do best: negotiate. What good is being a lawyer if I cannot use my talents when they are most needed, *non?*" He reached down beside him and lifted a slim black briefcase off the concrete. Balancing it on his lap, he flicked the latches, slipped a hand inside, and pulled out a set of documents.

When he had presented the package to her, Michele noted the extensive French text on the first page. "I really don't have time for this right now. What is this all about, and what does it have to do with me?" she demanded.

"It is what you came here for. I have convinced my family to make a *réparation* to you in the amount of one million Euros. From the company's charitable account. It is the most appropriate source, for all parties involved." He looked at her tellingly. "With the current exchange rate, this works out to approximately one and a half million Canadian dollars. It is all outlined in this agreement. I do have a copy here in English as well, and you will need to sign both the French and the English contracts. Then everything will be finalized. The funds can be in your account in a matter of days."

Michele was speechless. She tried to process what she'd heard but the meaning of Sébastien's words didn't immediately register. Reparations? Contracts? Did he really just say what she thought he had said? When she was able to speak again, she could manage only a shaky, "Um, what?"

Patiently, he explained it again, pointing out various sections and clauses. She could not look at them. The typed characters waited out of focus in her peripheral vision, impersonal and unfeeling, and she had the urge to push them away. Something didn't feel right.

"How—is this possible? Your grandfather was clear about not giving me anything, so this seems like an abrupt about-face here. I didn't exactly get the vibe that he was going to change his mind. Wait, is this his way of buying my silence?" She became agitated. "That's it, isn't it! He's trying to protect the precious Bouchard reputation and get that award, and you're helping him do it. You just want me to go away quietly. I should have guessed—"

"No, no, you are wrong. While bringing this subject to a close is certainly convenient for him, it is not the motivation for the decision. I simply offered him what he wanted: me." Sébastien gave her a melancholy smile.

His last sentence made her queasy. "What does that mean?"

"In exchange for his cooperation, I have agreed to come 'back to the fold' and become the permanent legal head for the company, as my grandfather always wanted. It did not take long for him to accept; in fact, he said that it was worth every *centime*. In his opinion it is a small price to pay to ensure the family legacy."

"What? Sébastien, no!"

"*Oui, ma belle.* It was the only way. I must tell you, the amount that you will receive is only a small portion of what would have been my great-uncle's estate, but I hope that it will be enough to put your mind at ease and allow you to move forward with your life."

This was it—Michele finally had what she wanted. Now that the purpose of her trip had been fulfilled, she could go back home and start fresh. It should be cause for celebration. So why did this victory feel so hollow? "But what about starting your own firm?"

In one motion Sébastien retrieved a pen from his inside pocket and pointed it to a blank line on the first page. "If you would please sign as indicated, beginning here ..."

Did he not hear me? I mean, maybe that's a good thing. In theory, I could just sign these papers and get out of here and all of this could be put to bed. Her eyes darted from the pen, to Sébastien, and back to the pen before she made her decision. She ripped the writing instrument out of his grasp and lowered it to the document. The silver tip hovered above the white space like an airplane waiting for clearance to land, but she would not give the go-ahead. She lay the pen down and let her hands go limp on the table. "I'm not signing anything until you answer my question. Right now."

"*Comme tu veux.* The firm was part of a beautiful dream," he started. "But dreams, they are not reality. Let me ask *you* a question: do you know why I chose the law as a profession?" Michele shook her head, and he continued. "It was the idea of studying the past in order to apply this knowledge to the present, share it with others, and in the end, to make society function more harmoniously ..."

His opening statement sounded like it could have been made by an archivist. Between her own work and her recent personal discoveries, Michele comprehended this sentiment better than anyone. She leaned forward and listened to him present his arguments.

"... To uphold the rules of our *République* while at the same time always analyzing and critiquing them to make life more fair for everyone. People think that the law is *ennuyeux*—boring—but I believe the classic philosophers when they wrote that knowledge is power." His shrug formed a natural and physical punctuation mark. "I began this career with much idealism, but the competition, it is harsh; I had to put away my *notions utopiques*—you understand?— in order to succeed. I told you in this very place that I had done terrible things to succeed, and I believe that some of my past choices would cause you to think differently about me. To stand with those that one knows with certainty are guilty or corrupt, it kills the soul over time. With my own firm I would have had the luxury of accepting or rejecting clients, following my conscience rather than my ambitions. This can no longer happen, but now I make a positive impact by a different means. By helping you, I can finally use my profession for good—just not in the way that I had planned."

She weighed his speech, examining his reasoning. History and law. She had not made the connection before but once Sébastien had talked about the two together, the interplay of passions in him was clear. They had been there the first time she'd met him, in fact, on the plane. She replayed the scene, this time watching it through the lens of emotion and experience. That book Sébastien had been reading had appeared so clinical, but in actuality it had said a lot about him if she'd only looked beyond the information on the surface. Why had she made so many assumptions about him? She had wasted precious time stuck in her head instead of engaging with life around her, and now she and Sébastien had only a few minutes left together. "Tell me about that book from the flight. It was about law."

"A classic text by Jean Brisseau on the history of French law; it influenced me greatly. *Monsieur* Brisseau was a lawyer, scholar, and historian and I have always admired his work. He dedicated his life to the science of law, taking the approach of beginning with studying the history on a regional basis. It was brilliant."

"This gives me a whole different take on your Paris tours, you know," Michele teased before becoming serious. "I wish I'd appreciated them more. I wish so many things were different. I don't want you to give up your dream for me." Her fingers tiptoed along the tabletop towards his.

He motioned behind him with a jerk of his head. "I have accepted my fate." The man in the suit jacket was hunched over his table, nursing a beer from a tall Kronenbourg 1664 glass. Around him the waiters bustled through the café attending to their customers, but they gave Suit Jacket Dude a wide berth as if he were toxic. Apparently, Michele observed, they knew better than to disturb him. She watched one young waiter venture closer only to be waved off with a grunt. "*Celui*, he is new here," Sébastien confirmed, reading her thoughts.

"Listen to me," she said. "You have so much to offer the world. Don't become that guy over there, spending every day sad and alone in the neighbourhood café. Don't lose who you are because of me. Think about your own future, and I'll figure out mine. You could still build a firm and do great things. I know you think you're doing the noble thing right now, but the terms you're agreeing to are crazy.

How are you going to feel about this a year from now? Ten years from now? Forever is a long time." Their hands were only a few inches apart.

"This is my penance for all of my misdeeds over the years. It could be worse. I will spend my days with my family. What is that saying? *Better the devil that you know?* They are difficult, and I rarely agree with them, but there will be no surprises. And it is guaranteed that I will be putting in long hours; the benefit being that I will be well-compensated, and I will not be here so often. As long as I keep working, I will not have the time to be sad and alone. I can take my comfort in knowing that you will be looked after."

His words echoed his great-uncle's as captured in Clotilde's diary over sixty years prior, and they jolted Michele. This must have been what it had felt like for her grandmother when she realized the lengths to which someone would go for her. True, unconditional, enduring devotion was a rare gift. Except her grandmother had lost Maurice, and Sébastien was right there in front of Michele, alive in body—but in danger of losing his spirit. She seized his hands and squeezed them.

"I can't let you do this, no matter how badly I need the money. I'm not going to lie: it would be a huge help right now. According to my landlady, I may end up homeless when I get back to Victoria, and I'm so far behind on my bill payments that I don't know how I can ever catch up. I haven't even bought school supplies for my son yet, and he's starting kindergarten in two weeks. But you know what? I have people I can ask for help, and I should've done that a long time ago. You don't have to be the one to pull me out of this situation I created."

Sébastien reversed the orientation of their hands, moving his to the outside. "Still you do not understand. From the moment that you took the seat next to me on the airplane, I have been attracted to you. Foolishly I did not make the best use of those hours over the Atlantic. In my defence, I did not want to make a poor impression, and I did not expect that we would see each other again—Paris, after all, has a population of over ten million residents. When I saw you at the Promenade the next morning, it was a surprise for me, and I would not take that second chance for granted. The initial attraction grew in a short time and developed into a relationship such as I have never before experienced." His eyes, now level with hers, glowed greener with a new intensity. Although the afternoon was again humid, it was Sébastien's breath that warmed Michele's cheeks.

"I don't know what to say," she whispered.

"Say that you will let me do this for you. Let me fix my family's grievous error." He reached for her face and smoothed a loose lock of hair back behind her ear.

She held back the desire to stroke his chin, visibly rough with the beginnings of a five o'clock shadow. "How am I supposed to just go home, knowing what all of this has cost you? Maybe I could stay longer. It doesn't feel right to leave you like this, not now. Isn't there anything I can do?"

"You can walk away. Think of your family and go home to your little boy. This is the best option. *Non*, it is the only one. Please. You and I, we cannot be together; we know this. Too much has occurred, and the wounds are still raw for everyone involved. Your energies are better spent in Victoria, where you can plan for the future. Remember, history is full of stories, but it is easy to get lost there. We can live in the past only for so long. Sooner or later we must return to our own time and place, and hope that we have brought forward something of value."

"But ..." Her protest was feeble. She knew he was right. Tears ran down her face, curling themselves over her jawline and down the sides of her neck. She forced a laugh, but it came out as a hiccup. "This is like one of your John Cusack movies, isn't it? Happy and sad at the same time?"

"Except that we are missing one vital scene." Sébastien angled his forehead until it touched hers and she closed her eyes. The point of contact pulsated, vibrations shooting out to every cell and nerve ending in Michele's body, and her network blazed—an internal City of Light. She was acutely aware of his palms pressing against her arms, caressing her skin on the way to her shoulders. With his thumbs he gathered the drops from her neck and followed them to their source. He stopped there under her temples and held her head with his fingers.

"*Regarde-moi.* I want to preserve this image of you for always. It is the last thing that I ask of you before you go."

Doing as he requested meant letting go of her own "beautiful dream"—not simply to be carefree and to have fun and adventure, as she had believed for so long—but also to find the right someone to share it with. *Dreams aren't reality; Sébastien said so. This has to end. We can't go on like this.* She opened her eyes.

"Michele, I love you." He tipped her chin up and their lips met. Patrons and passers-by melted into the sweltering Royale Pereire terrace, leaving her and Sébastien together under the red covers of the café awning. The bistro table, still as wobbly as it had been the first time, cheered them on.

CHAPTER 11

Circumstances and current events dictated that the ceremony be a simple one, yet still I felt like a queen. Though such an occasion is often described as a <u>beginning</u>, in these first days I have realized that it is rather a <u>returning</u>. Not so much as in going back to everyday practicalities such as cooking and cleaning (though I suppose the claim would be accurate), but of moving in a circle. It is odd, but I get the vague impression of having somehow been here before, and in this way, I know that I am precisely where I am meant to be.

The women of the church have been welcoming to me ever since I arrived here five years ago. After the wedding, they generously provided a small reception decorated with flowers from their lush gardens—the same flowers that were used for my bouquet. We cannot afford a honeymoon, of course, but in Philippe I have all that I could ever desire. Together we will create that which is most valuable in this life: traditions, memories, family ... a home.

* * *

Friday, August 21, 2009

Every piece of equipment was occupied, and the neighbourhood children flitted from slide to spring rocker to ladder. Even the green benches, which Michele had gotten used to finding vacant, were taken up by tired mothers and fathers, misshapen diaper bags, and picnic baskets laden with baguettes and fruit cut into pieces small enough for little mouths to consume. Given how late the French ate, it was no wonder those kids needed something to tide them over until dinner. It must have been close to five o'clock already, and that kind of rambunctiousness burned a lot of energy. It did for Henry, anyway, but the more he used up, the more he found. His spunk was endless—the great mystery of the young.

Michele, on the other hand, was still short-winded after taking off from the café, though more from emotional than physical exertion. Leaving had been agony, but she couldn't bear to stay either. Her instincts had taken over and she ran, never looking back. Now she rested against the black wrought iron fencing to catch her breath and think. Or better yet, to stop thinking.

At the climbing structure, a toddler pulled himself up to standing and took a few unsteady steps before landing hard. His cries were sharp as sirens. As his wails rose and fell, someone that must have been his mother rushed to him. Michele watched as the woman pulled two colourful bandages from her bag and applied them to each skinned knee. Like magic, the crying ceased and soon the boy again made his way back into the chaotic circuit.

I wish everything was that easy, she thought. There was no bandage big enough to fix what ailed her. The truth was, though, that what she really needed was the very opposite: to rip off her own Band-Aid and grow up. Take responsibility. Be a better mother. Other people's families would always be fascinating, but going forward she had to put more effort into her own. But first things first: book a flight out of France and return to Vancouver Island. *I really hope I can get one tonight. There's gotta be something.* She didn't have any experience with working the system and putting together an itinerary for air travel; this was a situation that required professional expertise. If Scott couldn't find her a way home right away, then no one could. He had gotten her here on short notice to begin with, after all, so maybe he would help her again.

Saying a silent last goodbye to the playground, Michele left through the gate. She moved at a good clip and reached the hotel a few minutes later. In her room, her suitcase and backpack were on standby just inside the door. They were ready for their next destination, and so was she. *Don't worry.* She patted the bag containing the diary pages. *We'll be back where we belong soon.*

She counted back on her fingers. It was after eight in the morning on the West Coast, so Amanda would be up; even in summertime, her children never slept in past seven. Amanda had once said it was the universe's little joke—a way of punishing her for having always been late for everything growing up. Barbara took great and obvious joy in this cosmic payback aimed at her daughter.

The phone rang four times and Michele was in the process of drafting a voicemail in her head when Amanda picked up.

"Hello?" High-pitched screams volleyed back and forth in the background, breaking up the call.

"Hey, it's me," Michele hollered over them.

"Michele? Hold on, I can hardly hear you. Don't hang up. Connor!" Amanda yelled in a muffled voice, covering the handset. "I'm on the phone! I swear I will throw that game in the garbage right now if you don't stop fighting over it! Can you just play nicely, please?" She returned to the conversation. "I'm sorry, go ahead."

Michele laughed out loud. "I see that mornings are still as fun as ever in your house."

"Ha. They're a riot. No, seriously though," she whispered. "They actually are for the most part, even though it's chaos all the time. Just don't tell my boys. I'm way outnumbered here already, and I can't give them an opening. They'll eat me alive!" Amanda raised her volume and continued. "But enough about me. How's it going in Paris? Did you accomplish what you were hoping to?"

"Uh ... well—"

"I mean, I'm not trying to pry. Who am I kidding? Yes, I am. I gave you space before, but I really want to know about this mysterious trip. Tell me everything."

Michele stared at the signed contract on the desk. She flashed back to the cold metal of the pen as Sébastien had placed it back between her fingers, his last touch committed to her memory. How could she even begin to explain the past week?

"I will, but not now. It's a really long story. What I *will* say though, is that we've got a lot of catching up to do, and not just about my trip." She paused, and when she spoke again her tone was softer. "It's been too long, and that's my fault."

"Hey, better late than never, right?" Amanda replied. "You know I'm ready whenever you are. Once you get back and caught up with things, I'd love to have a marathon chat. And—I might be pushing my luck here—maybe you and Henry could come to Kelowna for Thanksgiving this year?"

"You know what? I think that's a great idea. Consider this our R.S.V.P. But speaking of plans—" Michele changed the topic. "I'm coming back. So, I'm calling to see if you and Scott could book me a flight for as soon as possible? The two of you have already done a lot for me, but I'm asking for your help one more time. Give me the word and I'll leave for the airport; I'll take whatever's available. I just really want to be home."

"And I keep telling you we're happy to help. You know that with Scott's job, it's totally not a big deal at all. The tricky part will be finding you something for tonight. What time is it there?"

"Just after five in the afternoon."

"OK, well, let me just wrangle my *darling children* and I'll see what Scott can get you." Her boys had resumed arguing and Michele could practically hear Amanda rolling her eyes. "Anyway, are you sure you don't have any flight preferences?"

"No, book whatever. Just get me home, OK?"

"Alright, you've got it. Give me your number there and stand by!"

The ten minutes that followed crawled by at a snail's pace. When the phone rang, Michele pounced on it with the desperation of someone trapped on an island; her rescuer had arrived. "Amanda?"

"Hey, so do you want the good news or the bad news?"

"Please tell me you got me a flight!"

"That's the good news! But it doesn't leave for a bit, so you don't have to be at the airport for another three hours."

"Is that the bad news?" Michele asked.

"No. The bad news is that the only way to make this work was with multiple stops, and each one has a long layover. You'll get to enjoy the exotic locations of Amsterdam, Chicago, and Vancouver; and by that, I mean their airports. I'm sorry."

"What? Don't be. This is perfect, really. I'm already packed. All I have to do it check out of the hotel." Leaving the Magellan meant paying the bill for her stay, and all at once Michele remembered that Sébastien had said it would be a few days before she could access the Bouchard money. At this point she was still dependent on the generosity of others, though she planned to repay that debt a thousand times over as soon as she could. "I can't thank you enough for all of this. And I can absolutely guarantee that I will pay you back next week for the tickets and the hotel and whatever other expenses I've racked up."

Amanda sounded incredulous but accepting. "OK. I'm not

going to ask—yet—about where this sudden influx of cash has come from, but for now I'm going to assume it was through legal means."

"Ouch! Of course. I'm not some kind of criminal." Michele feigned offence.

"Well in that case, thank you. Just leave everything on the same credit card for now. We had already authorized the hotel to put all your charges through anyway. Get home safely, and we'll work out the rest later."

"There's one more thing." Michele fiddled with her necklace, looping it around her finger. "Like I said, I'll pay you back for everything. But before that, I'll be adding a very long, long-distance call to Da— ... to John."

After a pause Amanda responded. "You take as long as you need."

* * *

"Hey, it's me."

"Hi, honey. I've been thinking about you since our last chat, but I figured you needed space."

Michele made a note to start calling and visiting more often. Something else that needed to change in her life. "I'm OK. Really."

"I almost didn't pick up. Didn't recognize the number."

"Yeah, I'm not exactly at home right now ..."

"Oh, you at work? The call display is showing a whole lotta numbers right now. Very strange."

She heard rustling followed by a couple of beeps as he pressed different buttons. Classic John. "Don't worry about that. Am I coming through OK?"

"I'm always happy to hear from you, sweetheart, I told you. And

I can hear you just fine. Why wouldn't I be able to? It's not like you're calling from the other side of the world or something," he joked. "Anyway, how's that wonderful grandson of mine?"

"Uh, he's good. Great, actually. Excited to start school."

"I'm not surprised. He's a smart kid, just like his mom. Between Henry, all that great work you do at the archives, and," he paused, "the shock you had about your birth parents, you must have a lot on your mind. I worry about you. We don't talk that often."

That's being generous, Michele thought. She shouldn't have kept John and Barbara at arm's length all these years. Plus, her adoptive parents weren't getting any younger. "The important thing is that I'm calling now, isn't it? And yes, I've had a lot going on recently, but how are you guys doing?"

"Oh, you know us. We're just carrying on and enjoying our time together. It's a simple life, and that's just fine by us." The line between them went quiet. "Honey, as much as I love to chitchat with you, I get the feeling that there's some other reason for your call."

"You're right," she confessed, and she let the words spill out. "I'm sorry. I'm sorry for how I shut you down as a kid when you brought up my parents. It must have been so hard for you to respect their wishes when you probably wanted to tell me about them. And I'm sorry for my attitude when you finally did." She wiped her eyes. "You mentioned there was more. I didn't want to hear it then, but I'm finally ready. I want to know the rest. Tell me all of it. And don't stop until the end, no matter how awful the details might be."

Michele tried to brace herself for what was coming but the floodgates had already opened, creating a waterfall down her face.

"Alright. But first I want to say again how much your parents loved you, in their own ways. They were flawed, as you know. They were human. But they're a part of you. When you finally arrived, you had your dad's dark eyes and your mom's olive skin—Amanda was always a bit jealous of how you never got sun-burned, I think. Anyway, Edith thought you were just the sweetest little bundle of pink, so she went out and got you this pink stuffed rabbit that followed you everywhere until … until you figured out that they weren't coming back."

The bunny from her visions. It had been real too. A true recollection, not something she'd imagined. "There was a blue apron," Michele interrupted.

"There was. Now how on earth could you possibly remember that? You were still sittin' in a highchair then. I had no idea you had any memories from that time."

"I never said anything. I wasn't sure what to make of them, other than they scared me until very recently. But please finish. Tell me the rest."

"Well, one night, after the adoption was finalized and your dad left for good, your mom knocked on our front door. I guess you don't know this, but they lived just off Cloverdale Avenue, a few minutes' drive away from us. She'd come to say goodbye. Said it would be too painful to see you, so she wouldn't be coming around anymore, or going to Sacred Heart. Swore she was going to get a good job somewhere. I think we all hoped that one day you'd be reunited. She gave you a kiss and … that was the last time we ever saw her. It was raining buckets that night, and dark as all get out. The police said she'd been standing in the middle of Cloverdale. There was no way the driver could have seen her."

Michele cried into the phone, slumping to the floor. Her parents weren't a research inquiry or anonymous names on an old document. They were her family and they had lived real lives with the highs and lows that went with that. And now she knew.

"I'm sorry, honey. It's such an awful thing for a child to go through. Losing her mother, and Dan, and you … It broke Edith. No way she stepped in front of that car on purpose. She must have been distraught. As far as your dad, I don't know where Dan ended up. For all we know, he could still be out there somewhere. Barb and I, we tried our best. I'm sorry if we ever made you feel like less than the intelligent, beautiful person you are. We've always loved you and we're proud to call you one of our daughters."

"No, don't ever apologize for how you raised me," Michele said, sniffling. "You stepped up when it mattered most, and because of that I had a great childhood. Thank you, for everything. I love you … Dad."

* * *

Michele's suitcase cleared the threshold and the door closed behind her. The next place she slept would be in her own soft, comfortable bed, next to Henry's, in their perfectly imperfect little upstairs space above Mrs. Eliades. It didn't seem so cramped anymore, and Michele even looked forward to the noisy pipes, gnomes and all. Backpack on, she lifted the suitcase with both hands and carried it down to the lobby. She would need to ask about the shuttle bus, but if it couldn't come soon enough, she would have to find another way to get to the airport. *I guess I could take a taxi this time since I can afford it now, but that just feels weird.*

She plunked her bags on the floor. Then hearing a call of *"Mademoiselle"* repeated urgently several times, she followed the voice to the evening desk clerk, who was trying to flag someone down.

"Mademoiselle, I did not see you come in earlier. There is a message for you."

Wait, does he mean me? She checked around her to determine if he could have been addressing another guest, but she was the only one in the lobby. *"Moi?"*

"Oui. I have it right here." He held out the note for her and she walked over, wondering who would have left it. Sébastien? A tiny bubble of hope rose up in her but popped as soon as it reached her head. Unlikely. They had said everything at the Royal Pereire. But if not him, then whom? She unfolded the message. Graceful, curvy handwriting filled the hotel-branded sheet of notepaper. It was most definitely not from Sébastien.

Michele, it read. *I apologize for not being able to stay until you returned. I have a rendezvous of my own this evening with a very special gentleman. But I am anxious to find out how it went at the café. Whatever happened, good or bad, everything will work out as it should—though it may not be according to your preferred timeline. Trust your feelings, and the truth, and time.*

I am not certain how long I will be unavailable tonight. This will depend on how well the evening goes! (At this point, a happy face had been added, making Michele giggle.) *For this reason, we may not have the opportunity to speak until tomorrow. Regardless, please call me on my mobile at this number—and let me know the outcome. Your message will help me to pass the time until I receive the detailed report.*

Your French friend,
Maxine.

A smile stretched across her face and she reread the note. Of all the crazy things to come out of this journey, her relationship with

Maxine was the least complicated. Michele had a whole new level of appreciation for simple. It was highly underrated.

"*Excusez-moi*," she called to the clerk. "I'm checking out now, but I need to make a call first. Is there a phone I could use? It's a local number, I promise."

He pointed across the room. "Yes, there is a guest telephone in the lobby for this purpose, on the side table in the corner. If you would like, I can complete your check out on the computer so that everything will be ready when you have finished. Would you like to charge the credit card on file?"

"Um, yes, thank you. There should be some long-distance calls showing as well. Please put it all on the same card. Oh," she added, "would you also please book me a seat on the next available shuttle bus to the airport? I'd like to go as soon as possible." *Then I can pay Amanda back and never have to borrow money again. And it will be my turn to help out the people I love.* She pledged her silent vow and made her way to the phone table.

Just as Maxine had predicted, she didn't answer her cell. Michele had hoped to say goodbye in person, or at least in real time, before leaving Paris, but was forced to follow the instructions she'd been given and record a message.

"Hey, it's Michele. Your co-worker gave me your note. I'm guessing since I got your voicemail that your evening is going well, so congratulations! I wish I could've seen you, but I'm also really happy you're having a great time with someone you obviously care about. Anyhow, the café meeting with Sébastien was ... not what I expected at all. Too much to explain here, but I swear I'll fill you in. Let's just say that my *project* is now over so I'm going back to Victoria. I'm heading to the airport right now, in fact. Once I get settled at home, though, I'd love to chat. If you're up for a long-distance friendship, then I'm game. *Au revoir, mon amie*—for now."

As she hung up, she spotted a bus pulling up in front of the hotel.

"You are in luck, *Mademoiselle*, the shuttle has just arrived to drop off passengers and the driver has space for you," the clerk announced. "Do you need more time? I could inquire about the next one."

She sprang out of the chair, scooped up her bags, and made a beeline for the door. "No, this is perfect. Thanks again. And say hi to Maxine for me when you see her!"

* * *

As it turned out she had boarded the bus at the beginning of its round of drop-offs. Instead of going straight to the airport, the driver took Michele on a final tour of the city as he made stops at various hotels. Exhausted but excited passengers ready to begin their Paris adventures were gradually replaced by departing visitors forever changed by their experience. The route took her past some of the landmarks Sébastien had taken her to on his Vespa. As the bus wound its way in and out of traffic—much more slowly than the scooter had done—she left behind the Arc de Triomphe, the Eiffel Tower, Place de la Concorde, the Luxembourg Gardens. They had other guests to welcome now.

She cast her mind back to when she had first arrived and was shocked to realize it had been a mere three days earlier. Considering she hadn't come as a tourist, she had seen a lot thanks to Sébastien's condensed introduction. They'd really only scratched the surface, but now she had a great foundation on which to build a future trip. *Future trip? Would I really come back?* Her French, she admitted, was fully reactivated, but just in time to leave. It would be good to keep it up and even start teaching Henry a few words and phrases. The language, and this country, was part of their family history. Maybe she could do some research and find out the places in France where her grandparents had lived. She and Henry could take a true genealogical vacation together, one that was about discovery and not vengeance.

The bus crossed the Pont Neuf and continued north through Montmartre, where it made its last stop near Sacré-Cœur before accelerating out of the city limits and towards the airport. Dusk was still a couple of hours away, but the sun had begun its unhurried descent across the western sky. A few distant clouds hung about, as relaxed as the coffee-drinking customers on a Left Bank café terrace in late afternoon. Paris had never been on Michele's bucket list, but now that she'd had a taste of it, could she really remain satisfied with that one sip? There was still so much left to savour.

And then there was Sébastien. Was there a chance of ever seeing him again? She couldn't help thinking about him now that they would soon be half a world apart. When she landed at home tomorrow, or whatever day that worked out to be, he would probably be walking through the doors of Bouchard Financial, starting the first day of the rest of his life of obedience and servitude. He'd made his choice and she knew in her head she should move on, but it was exactly because of his choice that she wasn't sure she ever could. With him, three days had magnified into something like three meaningful years, and she would take thirty more without hesitation. She could not see the same calculation working with anyone else in the equation.

For now, the only math she had to do was figuring out time zones. She pulled her backpack up from her feet and took a folded piece of paper out of a pocket. According to Amanda, the shortest of

Michele's three layovers would be five hours, in Vancouver. Before she got there, however, she would have to spend several hours in Amsterdam and a whopping ten in Chicago on top of the actual time in the air. *What the heck am I going to do to keep myself occupied?* she asked herself. *Even I can only people-watch for so long. I'll pick up a book or something in the gift shop.* But she knew the in-flight entertainment in and of itself wouldn't be the issue. No, the biggest problem with her imminent thirty-odd hours of travel would be that on each leg, the wrong person would be sitting next to her.

* * *

"This is Captain Jones speaking. Just want to provide you with a quick update here."

Michele adjusted her seatbelt and dug her fingers into the blue plush seats. "I have a feeling I'm not in economy anymore," she said under her breath. Her well-to-do neighbour rolled his eyes and went back to his copy of the *New York Times*.

I can't believe Scott got me in First Class. He really didn't have to do that, but this is pretty nice. She didn't expect to engage in any conversation, but at least she would travel in comfort.

"Folks," the Captain droned on, "there are quite a few planes ahead of us this evening. We're number seven in the queue for takeoff. As soon as we get the go-ahead, we'll be taxiing to the runway and then we'll get you up and off to Amsterdam. So for now, just sit tight, and hopefully we'll be on our way shortly."

Her upgraded passenger status was not going to push her to any newspapers for high rollers and nothing available in the gift shop had inspired her. Instead, she'd decided on far better reading material already on hand.

Before she could retrieve it, though, the flight attendant cut in. "Would you care for a drink before takeoff?"

"Oh! I don't know ..."

Perhaps sensing her unfamiliarity with the mysterious section of the airplane beyond the curtain, the flight attendant explained, "We have a selection of wines and spirits, or if you prefer a mixed drink, simply let me know. Of course, it is all included for you. You may choose from anything that we carry."

"I see. Hmm, I'm not much of a drinker." Michele hummed and hawed when the answer came to her in the form of a memory from another flight. "Actually, I would love a glass of white wine. Preferably French."

"Excellent. I will bring it to you right away." He nodded before disappearing into the galley. While he was gone, Michele reached under the seat in front of her, opened her backpack, and pulled out her grandmother's photocopied diary. Once she'd checked that the tray was completely clean, she put the stack down and looked at the first page. Clotilde's name waved at her from inside the front cover, welcoming her back. Today was a homecoming, and what better place to start off from than where it had all begun.

"Your wine." The flight attendant presented her the glass. "You will need to return your seat tray to the upright position once we are ready for takeoff, but you are fine to use it for now."

"Of course. Thank you." She focused her gaze on the seat beside her, erased the businessman from the scene, and put Sébastien—the real Sébastien, the one she had met and not the shell who would be working for his grandfather—in his place. With a wink, she raised her glass and toasted him. *To your happiness. I hope you can find it, despite the way things look right now.* She wet her lips and then dared to add, *And I hope that by some miracle we'll meet again. I'd give anything for another city tour with you.*

She returned to the diary and read, careful to keep the wine at a safe distance. She would take her time, she decided. There was nothing but time to kill anyway until she got home. Long flights weren't her only reason to take it slow, however; Henry was too. Her grandmother's story, her mother's story, had to be shared with him, and Michele wanted to get it right. She'd learned from interacting with school groups at the archives that it could be hard to explain history to younger children. It wasn't that they couldn't understand. It just had to be told in words and images that met them where they were. Some details might have to wait until Henry was older, but as her dad had said, her son was a smart little guy. If anything, he would be the one to keep her on her toes with endless follow-up questions. His would be easier than Janice's, but Michele wanted to be ready. She would deal with the matter of her boss's questions later.

"Attention, passengers. This is your captain once again. That backlog is now cleared up and we're good to go. We'll be taking off in just a few minutes. Crew, please prepare the cabin for departure."

Uncertain as to what to do with her drink, she downed the rest of the wine and handed the empty glass back to the flight attendant before securing her tray. She set the pages on her lap, peered out the window, and waited while the wine painted an orange streak through her to match the changing sky outside. The engines fired up and the airplane taxied out, taking off without warning when it reached the runway. They were in the air.

She watched Paris grow faint below her. The sun lingered on the cusp of the horizon and cast the opposite side of the city into darkness. But in the growing twilight, the lights of the Eiffel Tower came on, twinkling and setting off a chain reaction along the boulevards. Everyone on the plane had access to the same show—not that the businessman was bothering to take it in—but she felt as if the City of Lights was giving her a personal send off. She smiled back and then resumed her reading. She had gone through the diary a hundred times before, but now it was with fresh eyes. It was amazing how different everything looked from a new point of view.

CHAPTER 12

As the green leaves feel a touch of red begin to glow on their cheeks with the anticipation of a new season, so too does a flush touch my features and send me spinning serenely to the ground. Familiar places gleam in the golden colours of autumn, brighter and lovelier than I can remember. Not even when I crossed the ocean from France did I experience such anticipation. The change in the air is undeniable.

I met someone today. Time did not pass while his grey eyes held mine; it paused in parallel layers, an eternity of pasts, presents, and futures meeting in one moment. In him I saw a world of contradictions: youth and experience, newness and familiarity, impulsiveness and caution. I loved before, but never truly understood its depths until now. Finally, I have arrived.

* * *

Sunday, August 23, 2009

"Thank you," Michele mustered as she exited the shuttle bus like a zombie. Just because she'd been away did not mean that she'd lost the Victoria habit of showing appreciation to the driver at the end of every trip. She'd always wondered if people did that in other cities, too, but was under the impression it was a local thing. Doing it now signalled to her brain, more than walking through the airport after landing had done, that she was really here. After over a day of travel, she was nearly home.

It was surreal to be standing in front of the Accent Inn again.

The last time she'd been there, it had been dark out—in more ways than one. Now the heavy curtain of night had lifted, and she walked into the morning sun. She dragged her suitcase around the corner of the building and through the motel's back parking lot to Alder Street. Maybe it was the severe jet lag making her delirious—taking the milk run from Europe could do that—but her neighbourhood had never looked more beautiful. As she absorbed everything around her, she didn't think about the long-gone fields and orchards of the Tolmie farm, or the houses that had lined Blanshard Street so long ago. For once she appreciated her community as it was right then and there, cars and concrete and all.

It wasn't Paris but it was hers—an alternate universe all her own. The places she had frequented most often on her trip had their counterparts here. The Accent Inn replaced the Hotel Magellan. Stone apartment blocks turned to West Coast wood construction. Instead of the Promenade playground, there was Rutledge Park. Nothing had changed while she'd been away, but to her everything appeared shiny and new.

She turned left. Up ahead on the right-hand side, one peaked roof rose above the rest and she sped up until she hit the front steps. With a foot on the first one, however, she veered off and followed the cut-through beside the house, pulling her suitcase with her. Would Rutledge Park look different too, after everything she had learned? Staying close to the building to avoid being seen through the windows, Michele crept around back. At the end of the path the playground equipment waited for the children to be set free for the day. She was sure they would start funnelling in any minute now. It was already eight o'clock and both kids and parents alike would probably be starting to get squirrelly inside. *I'll be quick,* she promised. *I've got a kid that I'm anxious to see too.*

She adjusted herself like an antenna seeking better reception and moved until she could see around the distant tree branches blocking her view. A pair of black eyes made contact with hers, and then the pink elephant gave her a comprehending nod. It knew her. It had been a place of refuge since she'd moved into the area as an adult, but maybe, she realized, it was because it had watched her from the beginning. Until that last phone call with her adoptive dad, she hadn't a clue she'd spent her first couple of years living off Cloverdale Avenue. (She added finding the address to her research list.) Maybe her parents had brought her here. Somewhere she had read that Rutley had been in the park since the 1960s and that the playground was developed in the late 1970s—well before she was born. How many times had they lifted her up and held her on his back? How many times had her father pushed her in the swing or her mother guided her down the slide? She had no idea, but she was pretty sure the elephant did.

She imagined herself with her parents, the three of them together like one of the happy families at the Promenade. Even though she couldn't remember those moments, she cherished them now. There were details she would never know: ordinary, day-to-day things that were not written down and facts that weren't recorded. She was confident she could locate the house, but those intangibles could not be researched. That was OK, though, and no one would be more surprised at this acceptance than she was as she left the park.

It wasn't like her family history was missing anymore—though she hadn't known for the longest time it was hers she'd been chasing. The revelations and events of the past week had provided her with literally a lifetime of information. It was more than enough to push her into the present, beginning with a little boy inside who'd been neglected long enough.

She prowled to the front of the house, but at the bottom of the stairs decided there was no reason to make a silent entrance. There was so much she needed to say, and she refused to hide any longer. In truth, Michele didn't want to. From that point on, she was ready to take whatever was coming to her. Some of it would not be easy. On the phone Henry had sounded content without her. Mrs. Eliades would definitely have a few, or many, choice words for her. And losing the job Michele loved was still a real possibility, especially tomorrow after she told Janice everything. Despite these likely scenarios she resolved to be fully present for all of it no matter what.

The stairs shook as her suitcase banged against them on the way up. At the top, she leaned it beside the door, took off her backpack, and dug in the pocket for her key. All at once the door flew open and Henry stood there with his hands on his hips, red-faced and ruffled in his Spider-Man pyjamas. Before she could react, he flung himself onto her like the superhero himself swinging from a web and then letting go.

"Oh. My. Goodness!" She gasped as he squeezed her neck.

"Mummy, Mummy, Mummy—you're home!"

His enthusiasm nearly made her cry. "Yes, I'm one-hundred percent here! And you have no idea how happy that makes me."

She pried him off her to examine and memorize his every line and curve, right down to the tiny, fuzzy hairs on his body. His eyes shone like moonstones. *How did I not notice before how perfect he is?* Inside and out, he was the result of a divine recipe that flawlessly mixed ingredients from an infinite number of sources. He had probably inherited his carefree manner from his great-grandfather, Philippe. Michele figured Clotilde had given Henry his strong sense of right and wrong. And maybe his grandmother Edith had been the one to impart empathy and kindness to him. They had all bestowed their gifts on him, sort of like the fairy godmothers had done for Aurora in *Sleeping Beauty*. Other traits would be harder to trace back to specific family members, but they were there. Henry was the human archives of all that history, but he was his own person at the same time. Michele understood it now: both parts—the past and the present—were important. You couldn't separate them.

She gave him another hug. "Why don't we go inside? You can tell me all about what you've been up to over the last few days."

"OK, let's go!" They got up and he led the way, his pudgy hand pulling her by the fingers.

The initial commotion had awoken Ares, who lumbered over to investigate what had disturbed his perpetual slumber. When he identified Michele, the folds above his eyes twitched. She wasn't sure if that meant he was pleased to see her, or irritated she'd made him get up. His range of expression was limited. "Is that all I get, huh?" She admonished the bloodhound and then squatted down to pet him. The contact elicited a tail wag and a string of drool. Michele shook her head and laughed to herself. "That's better, I think. I missed you too, you old grump."

"Mummy, Ares isn't grumpy. He's smart. You just need to know how to talk to him, that's all. Watch this." Henry turned to the dog and massaged behind his ears. "OK, remember what we learned? Mummy's home now just like we wanted, so you have to say hello. C'mon boy, speak!" On cue, Ares raised his nose and howled, suddenly animated. Henry jumped up and down squealing and clapping, which sent the dog into a frenzy of barking. It was the most active she'd ever seen the animal.

"OK, that's a really impressive trick. Thank you for showing me. But it's getting pretty loud so maybe we should—"

Just then Mrs. Eliades charged into the living room waving her arms around her head. "Ay, ay, ay, why you make such a racket, you crazy dog! You give me a headache now. What is the matter with you?"

"That was my fault, I'm sorry," Michele admitted. "Henry's a little bit excited right now."

Mrs. Eliades glowered. "You are finally back." Michele noticed the absence of the word "home." "Of course, the boy is excited. He missed his mother. Children need their parents."

The women faced off until Michele broke the ice. "I know. I mean, I *really* know. I owe you an explanation."

"You owe more than that, I tell you," Mrs. Eliades shot back.

"OK, I deserve that, and you're right. Could we talk? I'd rather not wait."

"Fine. But then I have so much to do. Is lot of work to clean this house," she complained. "You see? I clean other houses for my work, and then I come here and have to work more. *Nobody* help me."

"That's not true anymore. Things are going to change around here—for the better." The intrigued expression on Mrs. Eliades' face gave Michele hope. "Hey, Henry? Do you think you could take Ares out in the backyard for a little while? Maybe he would like to run around instead of sleeping all the time, especially now that he's up anyway. You can keep the pjs, but put on some shoes."

Mrs. Eliades bobbed her head in agreement, hunched over Henry, and patted his cheeks. "This is good. Ares is too lazy. You can help him to have more energy, yes, my boy? But you no can play if you hungry, and Didi made breakfast for you. There is a bowl with yogurt and fruit and some honey on top. You like it. Go, eat."

"OK, Didi." Henry nudged the dog towards the kitchen and then turned back. "Mummy, you're not going to leave again, are you?"

"No, I'm not going anywhere."

"You promise?"

"I promise."

Satisfied, Henry trotted off with Ares in tow. Mrs. Eliades had already lowered herself onto the couch, and Michele joined her.

Mrs. Eliades spoke first. "This situation in France with your family is resolved now?"

"It is. I found what I was looking for."

"Michele, I no understand why you went there. You told me some reasons on the phone, but it was so late and nothing make sense to me at the time. Why you leave your sweet boy and your job just like that?"

"That's a fair question." She struggled with how to explain. "All of this started when I found a diary from the 1940s at work. It had been hiding for a long time, I think, and there was no paperwork or anything with it. It was in French, which was super annoying at first, but it was from Victoria. The really weird part is that I had this intense *need* to find out who had written it. And I know this is what I do as part of my job, but this time it felt different. I was drawn to this book, yet I never in a million years would've guessed that it was directly connected to me."

"The war years." Mrs. Eliades jumped on the date, becoming solemn. "They were not easy. My mother never liked to talk about it. She pass away and she never tell me anything from that time."

Michele noticed the change in the older woman's demeanour and shuffled towards her, continuing to monitor Mrs. Eliades' mood. The subject of the war could be a trigger for people who had lived through it. "That was pretty common. It must have been so awful for families. World War Two tore so many of them apart. The person who wrote the diary, Clotilde, lost her husband. She was lucky enough to fall in love again, but that man, Maurice, died unexpectedly from a health condition."

"So sad, so sad," Mrs. Eliades lamented. "This lady was related to you?"

"Yes, eventually I learned she was my grandmother. And honestly, it really messed me up when I did. I grew up with my best friend. Her parents adopted me. I was told my birth parents were transients who had abandoned me, and I didn't want to know more. My family was just not something I concerned myself with."

Mrs. Eliades appeared horrified. "No family? But family is the most important thing in this life. It is all we have."

"Well, I know that *now*. Anyway, by the time the truth came out, I was already emotionally invested in the story. It turned out Maurice had been well off, which my grandmother didn't know until after he was gone. But even though he had wanted her to be looked after, they weren't married. Sorry." Michele eased up. "I know it's confusing."

"No, is OK. Why you no tell me all of this before? I no have a lot of school so I am not smart like that, but I can listen. Maybe you don't know this but since you move in with me you are like a daughter. My Dimitri and I," she observed a moment of silence, "we were not blessed with children. This was my great shame. Your boy is the closest that I have to a grandson."

"Wow." Michele latched onto the confession. "I'm—"

"You continue please." Mrs. Eliades composed herself, breaking the moment but moving closer.

"Um, alright," Michele continued, part of her still processing what she'd just heard. "In the end his greedy brother in France wouldn't give Clotilde anything and that decision—well, you could say it had a lasting impact. Money was an issue for my grandmother and mother, and as you know, it still is for me."

At the mention of money, Mrs. Eliades backed away again. "This is tough for you and I am sorry about that. I help you for so many years, but Michele, you know I also have bills to pay. The money does not grow in the trees. I have to protect myself too."

"I totally get it, and I have a lot to apologize for." Without thinking, she reached forward and took Mrs. Eliades' hands, surprising them both. "I didn't do it on purpose, but I took advantage of you, and it was wrong. I thought I was getting by on my own, but in reality I had a lot of help and you were a big part of that." She refilled her lungs and let the force of the air push the words out. "I haven't told you everything yet. A lot happened in Paris. At first, I was all about going after the money that I was convinced should be mine. Eventually I got some of it—which on its own is quite a significant sum—but only *after* I had learned a few valuable lessons, and by that point the money didn't have the same meaning. But now that I *do* have it, I want to use it for good. Obviously, I'm going to pay off the bills and the rent right away, but I'm talking about after that. I thought that maybe, if you were OK with it, I could help *you* for a change."

Mrs. Eliades let out a "tsk tsk" in opposition. "No, no, no, nothing else to do. You pay your share, and everything is OK. You know that even when I was so mad before, I no want you to move out. But now you have all this money, maybe you go to a nicer place ..." She looked around the room dramatically.

So this is what a motherly guilt trip feels like, and Greek style to boot. Michele tried to hide her smirk.

"It never crossed my mind, I swear. If I'm staying, though, what do you think about cutting back on the cleaning and slowing down? Or maybe renovating this place a bit? I'd love to do this for you. I mean, only if you want to. If you prefer to keep it the way you and

Dimitri had it, then I totally understand."

Mrs. Eliades stared at her, and then howled with laughter. "My Michele, I would love to spend more time with you and Henry and less washing floors. We will decide together what to fix here. It is your home, too."

* * *

Michele fought to keep her eyes open, but she had to force herself to stay up in order to adjust to the time change. Several times during the movie she had nodded off, but then Henry would change position and jostle her, which had been a good thing. Now as the credits rolled, her son snuggled closer and she embraced him tighter around his slight shoulders.

"So what do you think, kiddo? You tired yet?"

"No!" He yawned long and wide and stretched his limbs every which way before curling up against her again.

"I can see that. Just like Ares." When they had pressed play on the DVD player, the dog had sprawled out below them along the length of the couch like a draft stopper butted up against a door gap, and he hadn't moved since.

"Mummy, Ares sleeps more than me because he needs his beauty sleep."

She peered over the edge of the couch and counted the bloodhound's folds. "Right, of course. That seems like a reasonable explanation. Well, since you're not quite ready for bed yet, how about I tell you a story? It's a true story, and guess what?"

"What?" Henry's eyes were round as saucers.

"It's all about our family. I learned about them while I was away, and I thought you might like to learn about them too."

His face was serious. "I didn't know we had a family, Mummy. Just Auntie 'Manda, and Grandma and Grandpa."

"Everyone does, even us. The story of ours is kind of jumbled, but I think you'll be able to understand it. Just stop me if something is confusing, OK?"

Michele wove together the narrative, not methodically, but wherever the threads took her. She told her son about the strength of his great-grandmother and from there guided him through the complex tapestry of their history. Even though she omitted graphic details, she told the whole truth, both happy and sad. When she'd finished and answered every one of Henry's many thoughtful questions, she kissed his forehead.

"So even though we didn't know about them, our family was still part of us this whole time. They help to make us who we are, *even* if we don't know how. It's important to know where we come from." She got up and went to lift him off the sofa. "That's the end for now. Let's get you off to bed."

"But you missed someone," he whined. "What about my daddy? Did you find him too?"

"Oh." She sat back down. "Um, well, I don't know where he is." She hadn't anticipated that line of inquiry, but of course Henry would be curious about his father. *How am I going to explain a one-night stand with someone I never want to see again to a five-year-old?* "The thing is, I don't know where he is because I only met him one time." She tried to keep her tone light, but Henry's obvious disappointment was unbearable. This had to be about him and not her own issues. "But tell you what. If you want me to, I'll look for him for you. How's that sound?" *And maybe I'll look for my own while I'm at it.*

Henry's crushing hug said it all.

They climbed the stairs hand in hand and bid good night to Mrs.

Eliades, who as usual was still messing about in the kitchen.

"You have sweet dreams, my darlings," she cooed in time with Ella Fitzgerald and Louis Armstrong, the oldies station crackling in the background. With a gentle shove, Michele encouraged Henry up the rest of the way to their room and then hung back, unobserved, on the oak steps. Mrs. Eliades layered towel upon towel over the plastic basin on the chair. There would be fresh bread with breakfast in the morning, and it would taste a lot better than an everything bagel. Once the dough had been tucked in to rest, Mrs. Eliades cleaned the counter, swinging her wide hips from side to side as she did so. The music faded out, and she took the break between songs to pick up the framed photograph of her husband, dust it off with the edge of her apron, and return it to its place.

They must have had some wonderful dances in that kitchen. Just like me and my mother must have had some fun in ours. Michele saw the highchair and the blue apron. She heard the singing.

At that moment, the next song came on the radio and it called her name. It was the same "Michelle" as always, and yet a new version; not bringing unwelcome nightmares, but lovely memories instead. She tapped the railing to the beat and hummed along. It would have been a shame to rush over and turn it off. After all, lyrics like those were universal. The only thing to do was let them play through.

* * *

Monday, August 24, 2009

"Well, here goes." Michele opened the door to the archives and went in. Whatever her fate, she was ready for it. Carrying a stack of pages, she skipped past the bookshelves and tables to the reference desk where Janice was switching on the computer.

"You're back!" her boss exclaimed, getting up. "I wasn't sure you would be here this week. Is your family alright?"

"They are. My time away really—brought us closer together."

"Michele, that's fantastic. I'm so glad everything worked out. I know it's selfish, but I'm also relieved that you're here. It's been busy ever since you left. Some of those fall researchers are apparently getting an early start this year."

"You are not selfish, trust me. And I'm thrilled to be here—you have no idea how much. But you'll probably feel something other than relief when you hear what I have to say."

Janice came around the desk. "That sounds ominous. You're not quitting, are you? I know things are up in the air with your job, but if you can just ride it out for a little while—"

"No, it's not that," she interrupted. "I'll stay as long as you'll have me. But I need to show you something first." Michele set down the copied diary pages. "It's about that discovery I made. I haven't been honest with you."

Janice bent over the pages but didn't seem to recognize them. Clearly she hadn't looked at the original while Michele was away. "What's this?"

"A lot more than it seems. It's a copy of the diary I found. Here, you see this name inside the front cover?" Michele pointed it out and explained, using the diary itself as a prompt. "I'm sorry I didn't loop you in. Especially after you gave me a key and let me do all that research. You're the archivist. And my boss. I should have told you as soon as I knew."

"This is your family?" Janice asked for the second time. "That's amazing! But why on earth didn't you say anything? Why didn't you tell me you were going to Paris, and the reason for it? You didn't need to hide it from me. I would have understood."

"I know. I shouldn't have lied to you about the trip, and my connection to the diary. I couldn't get past all of this until I told you everything. Please don't report me to HR. I promise I won't come back if you don't want me to, even though I love this work so, so much. But there's just one more thing."

"Really, Michele, what else could there possibly be?" Her boss sounded exasperated.

"Since there's no paperwork for the diary and I'm *technically* the direct descendant of the person who created it, I thought I could sign a gift form and make the donation official. Then I'll go. I just want to make sure my grandmother's story is protected."

Janice closed her eyes and let her head drop. The hands on the wall clock ticked along, oblivious to the drama below. Michele counted their jerky hops once around the white face while her boss deliberated.

"If you need more time to think everything through, or if you just can't trust me anymore, that's fine. I'll just be going, then—" Michele threw her backpack over her shoulder.

"No, wait," Janice stopped her, her eyes glassy and her voice faltering.

Michele did as she was told and then held her breath. She placed a bet with herself as to how long it would take to hear the words "You're fired." Her money was on ten seconds.

"Taking off like that—lying about it—was wrong. There's no denying that. At the same time, you've acknowledged your poor choice and taken responsibility. You could've easily withheld the truth about the diary and I would never have been the wiser, but you didn't. And given the extenuating circumstances and what must have been a difficult childhood for you, I can understand why you did it even if I don't agree with your actions. If you had just come to me with this right from the beginning, I would have had no problem at all. I could have helped you find the truth."

Had it been ten seconds yet? Michele had lost count, but the natural pause seemed like the logical time for the axe to fall.

Janice pressed on. "You are probably the best employee I've ever had. You're detailed, and conscientious, and passionate. The researchers love you. So much so, in fact, that they may have helped you in terms of your job."

"What do you mean? How does this relate to you letting me go?"

"Michele, what I'm trying to say is that I'm not letting you go. You had a lapse in judgement, but you're good at what you do—and now the decision makers at the city know it. Remember how I said that we're supposed to spend less time on inquiries? Well, I'm glad that you don't. While you were away, a number of researchers who you assisted recently sent in glowing letters about you. They went on and on about how wonderful you were and how you had gone above and beyond for them."

Michele blushed. "Really? Wow."

"Yes, your biggest fan was someone named Daphne. She said you found her grandparents for her? Something like that. Anyway, I forwarded these on to management and they were impressed. They'll take the feedback into consideration. Nothing definite yet, but there's a chance you could keep your hours after all."

"So, does this mean—?" Michele ventured.

Janice beat her to the bottom line. "Let's get something straight. No more secrets, alright? As long as nothing like this happens again—ever—then I'd really like you to stick around."

"I can do that." And Michele meant it.

* * *

Saturday, August 7, 2010

Water bottles: check. Sunscreen: check. Snack bars: check. What am I forgetting? Michele searched the blue and red striped tote bag, trying to jog her memory. They weren't going far, of course; if they needed something they could just come back and grab it. But that wasn't the point. She wanted to enjoy their day at the park without interruption. "Are you ready, *mon chéri*? Let's go before it gets too hot out!"

She sat cross-legged on the floor near the front window, basking in the sunlight as she packed. The first half of summer had been glorious. Every spare moment had been spent outdoors at a playground, with a picnic, along the water, or some combination of the three. The regular fresh air and exercise had done them both a world of good. She hopped up and stuck her arm through the handles. "You coming?"

"Yes, I was just getting a few things!" The thump of approaching feet heralded Henry, who appeared carrying a dump truck and a child-sized bucket. "I'm bringing these to play in the rocks!"

"I knew we were missing something." She added the toys to the other essentials. "Oh wait, you don't have your hat!"

"Mummy, do I have to wear one?" her son griped.

She took his sun hat off the hook and dropped it on his head. "Yes, you sure do. Do you remember how to say *hat*?"

He scrunched up his face. "Is it—*chapeau*?"

"*Oui! Très bien.* Your French is coming along nicely. Soon you'll be ready for our big trip." She directed him through the kitchen and out the back door.

"But *when* will that be? I wanna go now!"

"Not yet. But don't worry, France will be here before you know it. Now, who's gonna get to the playground first?"

"Me, me, me!"

They raced through the still-damp, fragrant grass. She slowed down to let him pull ahead, and then pretended to make a valiant effort to catch up. "I'm coming to get you! You're so fast though. Are you sure you're Spider-Man and not the Flash?" She lunged at him, picked him up, and spun him around until they both fell down in a heap, sending the bag flying. "OK, I think you win. You're almost too big for me to lift! Why don't you take your truck onto the gravel and play? I'll be there in a minute."

She bent down and pushed the rest of the strewn items back into the tote. When she got up, she put her hands on her lower back and stretched it out. *I'm going to have to stay fit to keep up with him. But he's the best motivation.*

At the playground, Henry was already busy building a maze of roads. She strolled over and while she admired his work, she noticed a subtle movement out of the corner of her eye. They weren't alone. Between the chains of a swing, she saw a man sitting on the pink elephant. *Has he been there the whole time?*

There was no one else around, so why was that guy up there? Clearly, he wasn't a parent. Mind you, she didn't want to judge. She'd had her fair share of thinking sessions on Rutley, but those were generally at night. *Maybe I should go say hello and check him out, just in case I need to report him to the authorities later.* Keeping her son in her sights, she zigzagged around the playground equipment and then looked up at the stranger. Except, she realized as the air was knocked out of her, he wasn't.

"It is about time that you showed up, *ma petite*. I have been waiting for hours."

Michele rubbed her eyes. It had to be a dream. "Sébastien?"

He jumped down beside her and brushed pine tree needles from his pants. "Ah, I am relieved that you remember my name. This is a positive start to our reunion, *non*?

"I'm ... I ..." She stuttered before spitting out, "How are you here right now?"

"The same way that you came to Paris a year ago. *En avion.* Flying really is the most efficient method." He stuck his hands in his pockets and wandered towards the walkway.

She tripped her way behind him. "No, you know what I mean. With the way things ended, I doubted we would ever see each other again. Not that I didn't think about it regularly."

He halted and turned to her. She didn't know how, but he seemed like himself again. Maybe working for his grandfather had agreed with him after all.

"That day was the most difficult of my life. Every morning after that was *sombre.* I resented my family and detested going to the office. But then I would picture you to remind myself of the reason I was there, and it gave me strength. I kept my part of the deal and did my work diligently, but still I was miserable and my family could see this. My mood penetrated even their icy hearts. The fact that the company received the Bank of the Year award also helped my case. The result is that we have brokered a new deal."

"OK. And I take it that it's a significant improvement on the last one?"

"*Absolument.* I am now free to start my firm—the process is already underway—and I will assist Bouchard on a consultant basis only, primarily with its charitable endeavours. This is, as you say, the best of both worlds. I can choose the matters that I would like to handle, and not involve myself in anything that I feel would go against my ethics."

"What? That's amazing! I'm so happy for you." Michele pushed her hair behind her ear. The temperature was rising quicker today than she'd thought it would. "Things have improved a lot for me too. Work at the archives is great, and I'm spending a lot of time with my son. That's Henry over there. I can't believe he's six already."

Sébastien followed her gaze. "I hope that you will introduce us, if you do not object."

"Yeah, I think you two could have a lot of fun together." As they walked towards Henry's rock piles, she jumped back to something nagging at her. "Wait, you still haven't told me what you're doing here."

Without missing a step, he took her hand. "You have already forgotten the lessons that I taught you. It is the time of *les vacances*. I did not feel that I had satisfied my curiosity for Canada—and Canadians," he added with a wink. "However, instead of registering for another boring conference, I put my focus on the recreation this year. You had told me much about your park and your neighbourhood, so I decided to come and see them for myself. It seemed only fair since you had visited mine."

"Yes. That's a reasonable argument." Michele stopped to find Sébastien had shrugged after his statement and it hung in the air as if he were awaiting a verdict. She smiled and pulled him in. "Then in that case, let me show you around."

Author Bio

Sonia Nicholson has worked in archives for fifteen years. A first generation Canadian who grew up in a Portuguese immigrant family in Osoyoos, British Columbia, Canada, she went on to study French and Spanish at the University of Victoria. She remained in Victoria and lives there with her husband, two children, and two rescue dogs. She's been to France several times, and just might be a bit obsessed with the country and culture. Her work has appeared in various publications including *Inspirelle*, *Literary Heist*, and *Pinhole Poetry*.